i don't
live here
anymore

i don't live here anymore

Gabi Kreslehner

TRANSLATED BY
SHELLEY TANAKA

Groundwood Books
House of Anansi Press
Toronto / Berkeley

First published in German as *Charlottes Traum* by Gabi Kreslehner
Copyright © 2009 Beltz & Gelberg in der Verlagsgruppe Beltz, Weinheim/Basel
First published in English translation in Canada and the USA
by Groundwood Books in 2015
English translation copyright © 2015 by Shelley Tanaka

Groundwood Books / House of Anansi Press
110 Spadina Avenue, Suite 801, Toronto, Ontario M5V 2K4
or c/o Publishers Group West
1700 Fourth Street, Berkeley, CA 94710

With the participation of the Government of Canada
Avec la participation du gouvernement du Canada | Canadä

 The translation of this work was supported by a grant
from the Goethe-Institut, which is funded by the German
Ministry of Foreign Affairs.

Library and Archives Canada Cataloguing in Publication
Kreslehner, Gabi
[Charlottes Traum. English]
I don't live here anymore / written by Gabi Kreslehner; translated by
Shelley Tanaka.
Translation of: Charlottes Traum.
ISBN 978-1-55498-803-7 (bound).
I. Tanaka, Shelley, translator II. Title. III. Title: Charlottes Traum.
English.
PT2711.R47C4313 2015   j833'.92   C2015-900061-0

Jacket illustration by Aimée Sicuro
Design by Michael Solomon

Groundwood Books is committed to protecting our natural environment. As part
of our efforts, the interior of this book is printed on paper that contains 100% post-
consumer recycled fibers, is acid-free and is processed chlorine-free.

Printed and bound in Canada

MIX
Paper from
responsible sources
FSC
www.fsc.org   FSC® C016245

For Martin and Katharina

I don't live here anymore.

Shit, it's true. I don't live here anymore, and anyone who says anything else is lying. But no one does say anything else, because there's nothing else to say. It's just what it is. I don't live here anymore.

Sometimes I still come here, to our house, our garden. If Mrs. Springer sees me, she waves, but only a tiny one, kind of careful and nervous. She's the one who lives here now with her husband and their kid, and she probably has a guilty conscience, because she for sure knows that really, this is my house.

By the way, Mrs. Springer is quite a beautiful woman, one most people wouldn't mind having for a mother, to show off on parent-teacher night, make everyone's jaws drop. She's delicate and blonde, like a fluffy pastry from an expensive bakery.

My mother is more like a yeast bun. Not bad, but something you can get in any old supermarket.

So. Our house. Now the Springers are there and he can't stand me and he's already shooed me away like I'm some mangy dog or a stray cat. "Quit bothering us! Don't keep coming around. Go home! You don't live here anymore!"

And then he got all red and puffy like a big rubber ball, and I looked at him and hoped maybe he'd pop a spring or two himself, but he didn't. He raised his hand and started coming toward me, and that's when I realized that I was actually making my way up to the door.

Besides, he's right. I don't live here anymore. And when you're right, you're right, and that's not his fault.

By the way, my name is Charlotte, and it all started a year or so ago.

∾

We had a patio at home and Mum had a bikini, shiny and golden yellow, and we had this neighbor, Melchior, and the sight of Mum in her bikini had a very special effect on Melchior. He was right there ready to launch like a guided missile. You could set your clock by him.

No sooner was she lying there lolling around in all her yellow-gold bikini glory than there he was. Standing beside her lounge chair whispering away. Asking whether she was thirsty. And she should really come and use his new pool and why not and it would make him soooo happy if she did. "Silvia! Come! Be my angel!"

It was embarrassing. Just not to her. She went. She was thirsty, it was hot, she wanted a swim and his backyard was so wonderfully cool. He was very persuasive.

Melchior was a real ladies' man. Every weekend he'd bring one home, some slick city woman, the ones with legs that go at least up to their armpits. My parents would stand at the kitchen window and peer over and shake their heads, and Dad would say how Melchior was such a playboy, like really, and that Mum should watch out, like seriously, because she was a real bombshell in that yellow bikini, and that Melchior for sure had the hots for her, for her and that figure of hers, any blind man could see that.

Mum smiled, kind of flattered.

"You're crazy!" she said. "You're out of your mind! How deluded you are. Besides, I always have the children with me."

"Oh, yeah?" he said. "Is that so? Is it, Charlotte? Do you keep an eye on your mother? You don't let her out of your sight?"

No, I didn't let her out of my sight. Of course not. Of course I kept an eye on my mother. Because of her hot bod. Because of Melchior. Because Dad wanted me to.

Because I was an idiot. Because I had it all wrong.

Because it was Dad all along.

Boy, was it ever.

৵

We left. Immediately.

They screamed at each other. She called him an asshole and then he yelled. You don't forget something like that. And yet it all started completely innocently.

"What's this?" she asked him, holding something up by her fingertips.

"Oh … that. It belongs to Babsi. Give it to me and I'll take it to her." And he held out his hand, all innocent.

But she wouldn't let him get away with it.

"Babsi who?" she asked, and suddenly it was clear that she knew everything.

As she got us packed up, me and my brothers, she was as white as a sheet. She put us in the car, and when we drove past our garden I saw the elm tree that towered up outside the window to my room, the one that wafted cool breezes in summer and snow in the winter. My special wishing tree.

I felt tears on my face as we drove away from our former life. I saw the house getting smaller and smaller, and my tree disappeared and the summery green of its leaves gradually turned this nothing shade of gray, and I knew for absolute sure that this was it and that it was more likely that my mother's favorite ringlotte plums would start to grow on my wishing tree than that we would ever come back and be together with our father again.

We were driving to our grandmother's, and she would take us in and we would stay there.

"That's the way it is with these corporate types," she said to my mother that first evening. "Welcome to the club. Come, dear, put the kids down and let's have a glass of wine."

I did not go down. After all, I was almost fifteen and not a kid anymore. I sat outside the door and eavesdropped.

Mum said it had nothing to do with being a businessman. She said that was crazy, and Grandma should quit thinking that right now. Grandma said Dad was probably going through a midlife crisis and that Mum shouldn't be too sad because things would sort themselves out.

That's when I got my hopes up, and I got out my phone to do some texting, but then Mum started to talk, and her voice was soft and shaky, and I started to pay attention again.

"There is no more love," she said. "No more love between me and Max."

That's what she said. There was just no more love and that it didn't really have that much to do with Babsi.

Then it got very quiet in the living room for a long time, and I held my breath so that they couldn't hear me breathing, and I got hot and cold and I lay on the tile floor in the hall and thought that maybe my heart would stop beating and I would die.

The love was just gone, Mum whispered. That's why she was so sad, sadder than she'd ever been. Because she'd believed that the love would be there forever, always, for her whole life. And how awful it was to suddenly realize that there was nothing there but an emptiness that grew bigger and bigger and ate everything like a giant garbage disposal. Everything she'd once believed, that it would last a lifetime and beyond. That it could be like that.

I could feel my heart thumping hard and fast in my neck. It wouldn't be beating this fast, I thought, if I was dying, even if everything around me was falling apart.

Goddamn love business, I thought. Love sucks.

"Come, Charlotte," Mum called suddenly. She was standing in the doorway and she had her arms open and they were as warm and soft as ever, and she smiled at me in the middle of all the crying and that was the first time I ever wanted her to call me her Ringlotte.

∾

It's because once we were at a farmers' market, and there were fruits and vegetables as far as the eye could see.

We were walking past the stands and suddenly Mum flipped out.

"Ringlotte!" she cried. "They have ringlotte!" And before anyone could stop her, she stuffed a couple of these yellowy-red plums in her mouth.

"We'll take ten kilos," she told the market woman.

"Ten kilos!" Dad's jaw dropped. "Ten kilos of those funny things? Are you crazy? Who's going to —"

But you don't argue with Mum when she gets like this.

Over the next few days she stood in the kitchen and pitted and ate and pitted and ate and made jam and baked cakes and was happy.

In the evening she came up to my room, snuggled up to me and smelled like plum jam.

"You know," she said, "when I was your age, we lived in the country with my grandmother, in a big old stone house. In the garden there were ringlotte bushes, full of these greengage plums. For half the summer we ate ringlotte. A lot of them."

"Are we going to go there?" I asked.

She shook her head and smiled. "It's very far," she said. "And it belongs to another life. I don't even know whether the house is still standing. We moved into the city because my father got a job there. And my grandmother was old and she died soon after, and the house was sold."

"Will we go there anyway?"

She hugged me so tight then that I squealed.

"Well, we'll see, my Charlotte. My Charlotte Ringlotte."

And that's how I got my nickname.

And now that everything in our life has changed, now that we've left Dad and our house and my tree?

Now I liked it when she called me Charlotte Ringlotte.

It was like my comfort food. Better than scarfing down a bar of chocolate. Her voice trembled a little then, and I knew she had to swallow a couple of tears. But only a couple.

After all, she was brave, and she was grownup already.

And I was, too.

∽

After we moved into Grandma's, it was crowded. There were just too many of us.

Oliver and Felix hunkered down in Uncle Bert's room. That didn't bother anyone, least of all Uncle Bert, since he was off in America building a career, and probably wouldn't miss the room he'd had as a kid.

I got Mum's old room. As we stood in the doorway, a suitcase in each hand, she sighed.

"You know, Charlotte, it's like I've been plunged back into my childhood. It's sort of funny."

But it wasn't the least bit funny.

The lamp under the bookshelf threw out a pale circle of light. I took Mum's hand and pulled her over to the bed and we sat there and looked around her room.

"Mum," I said. "Aren't we going back again ever?"

She looked at me for a long time. Then she shook her head. "No. Probably not."

And that was it. At some point she stood up, went over to the window, pulled the curtains closed.

"Yuck! These are absolutely filthy. We have to wash them."

That's what we did the next day. I pulled down the big green heavy curtains and Grandma stuck them in the washing machine and then we hung them back up to dry.

The boys were running around the garden for the benefit of the neighbors, begging like poor little orphans.

"Mum," I said. "You don't have to go out to work. Just let the boys do their thing on the street. They'll make money hand over fist."

But Mum just gave me the finger. She'd completely lost her sense of humor, and that evening Felix threw up, the little jerk, after he stuffed himself with his entire stash — two chocolate bars, a pack of gummi bears and six sticks of chewing gum.

∽

The witch's name was Barbara, and she was Dad's assistant.

If only she were stupid and ugly and toady. And mean. And some kind of freak.

Unfortunately she wasn't any of those things. Unfortunately we'd met her before and we already knew her and liked her.

She was always super friendly whenever we visited Dad at his office. She chatted to me and Oliver about school and talked to Felix about kindergarten and asked us what we wanted for Christmas and where we were going for the summer and how she'd love to come and visit us because we were such great kids and our father was so lucky to have us. And whenever she bent over, a scent would waft out. It smelled like springtime and flowers, and you wanted to lean in to sniff it.

Everyone called her Babsi, and she was just like you'd imagine a Babsi. Sweet. And nice.

And so right from the start, you couldn't hate her. Besides, there was no getting around the fact that Dad was totally crazy about her and that was all there was to it.

Of course we wished that she were on the far side of the moon. And of course we would have loved to hate her. Really. But it wasn't happening.

Mum had nothing left anymore. No house, no husband, not even a real bed. Just a living-room couch.

And at first that's where she spent all her time,
lying there and watching TV, from *Grey's Anatomy*
to the Gilmores. Watching and eating anything she
could get her hands on — sour pickles, sweet tarts,
chips, whatever.

If my brothers came to her with their heads smashed
in, she'd point to me and say, "Go see Charlotte. She'll
take care of it. Right, Charlotte? That's my big girl!"

But I didn't. I took off. Out of the neighborhood,
through the streets, across the field, back to our house.

That's where I could be sad. And mad.

Thank God she soon pulled herself together, and
then she decided that our situation wasn't that tragic
after all, that stuff like this happened all the time, but
that from now on I had to look after my brothers.
Because she started working again, which was a dis-
traction for her, and she figured that was the end of my
freedom.

My brothers acted like idiots, just doing whatever
they wanted. Felix had just turned five and was still
going to kindergarten. Oliver was nine and going to
regular school, but just until one.

So goodbye to my sweet life!

When I got home after school, I had the boys on my
case asking for Dad, but Dad wasn't there, just me.

And when Mum came home in the evening and took over looking after Oliver and Felix, I still had all my homework to do.

It was shit.

∾

Anyway, the school thing got tricky. I wasn't moved on this past fall. I'd never been what you'd call a genius, much to the disappointment of my parents, but after we moved I just didn't have time anymore. In the end I had to help Grandma and then there were my brothers and I had to help Oliver with his homework and then Dad would want to see us and getting to school suddenly took twice as long and ...

And that was enough to send things straight downhill and pretty soon I'd had enough, too, and I had to repeat the year.

I didn't blame the teachers. "Charlotte," they would say, full of understanding. "Charlotte, we know you're going through a difficult time, but ..."

And then they'd beg me to do my homework so I could learn, because one simply had to learn and such was life and whatever, blah-blah-blah.

Ms. Meier-Wutschnigg told me about her own experience, when her parents divorced thirty or fifty or seventy years ago. I sat there and she looked at me and

I stared at the weird pimple on her nose and suddenly I couldn't help laughing.

She wrinkled her forehead and said, "Well, you're a strange one!"

I shrugged and thought, what do I care about your parents, you pimple-faced old bag?

Behind me people started to mumble and whisper, and I wondered for a second if I'd said it out loud.

But I hadn't. Thank God. I thought for a moment and asked, "Did they fight?"

"Who?" Meier-Wutschnigg asked, surprised.

"Your parents!"

She didn't know what to say.

"I believe she called him an asshole," she said.

She looked at me, nodded briefly. And we never talked about divorce again.

∾

"Wow," said Dani from my old class, after I told her about all this. I kicked at the stones in front of me, ran on ahead.

"Hey!" she called. "What's the matter? Are you crazy?"

So I stopped and she crashed into the back of me.

"I'm sorry!" I said. "Sorry. I never should have said anything. To you, and to Meier-Wutschnigg especially. I just wish my mother weren't always so …"

Suddenly I felt my throat and nose fill up and I kept gulping and gulping. And Dani was there and she gave me a tissue and just stayed with me.

"Yeah," she said softly. "In the end he screwed all of you."

We sat down on a park bench and watched the pigeons. They were pecking at little breadcrumbs, cooing and flapping around here and there.

"Do you think they'll get divorced?"

I shrugged and thought about what Mum had said, back when I was eavesdropping just after we arrived at Grandma's.

"I don't know. Yes. Probably soon. Doesn't everyone?"

I felt the tears come again, from my belly up into my throat. Shit, I thought. I don't want to cry now. Am I a baby, or what?

I jumped up from the bench right in the middle of the pigeons and shooed them all away.

Then we laughed, loud and sharp.

We kept walking, through the city, over the highway. To H&M. Tried on clothes and left them behind in the change rooms. Then back on the streetcar. Stopped for something to eat. Guzzled down a cola. And wrapped crunchy lettuce leaves in soft pitas and felt squishy slices of tomato between our teeth.

It felt good. And Dani's quick kiss on my cheek. And her hug. That, too.

∾

They got a divorce. Of course. It happened so fast, we hardly even noticed. Mum got dressed up before she left the house, and Grandma wished her luck.

I was sitting on the upstairs landing. Of course I knew what day it was. She'd told me the week before and Dad had muttered about it over the phone, the coward.

When she got home that evening, she was a little green around the gills.

She sank down onto the living-room couch, pulled me to her and said, "Now we're divorced, Charlotte."

I shook her off.

"How nice for you," I said.

Three days later I had my fifteenth birthday. A huge package arrived from Dad. Guilty conscience. It was a TV. Unfortunately I slipped when I was pulling it out and it cracked against the table and busted.

Too bad.

∾

I was the new class idiot, the super dummy. They didn't like me. They were already divided up in their tight little cliques. There was no room for anyone new.

First of all there was Sulzer and his groupies. Whatever he said was law. Even though a lot of people couldn't stand him, he was hot looking and that counted for something. Besides, he terrorized the teachers, because he could interrupt the class at any moment. He would stand up abruptly, go to the window and go into a loud commentary about the weather or whatever else he felt like. He would just yell across the room to one of the other kids in the class. He was a real asshole. He'd pick fights if he didn't like the stuff we were studying.

Mind you, he knew the teachers weren't too keen on him, either, and sometimes they would just kick him out.

Not that he cared, or that his behavior improved or anything, but at least the teachers had some peace, and so did the rest of us.

After Sulzer came the bitchfaces. Yvonne, Vanessa and whoever. They'd go out to buy pink underwear, whine about what a drag it was to have to wear braces, leave hair from their brushes all over the place and fawn over the Pussycat Dolls. They made fun of Sulzer a lot, because he was a bit on the heavy side.

"So, Sulzer, too many liverwurst buns?" Or, "Hungry again already, Sulzer? Not going to make it till lunchtime?"

But he'd just give them a look and that shut them up.

I admired that, because I couldn't manage it myself.

"Hey, you," they'd say, gathering around me and sneering. "Not a lot going on between the ears, eh? Taking the same grade over again! Way to go!"

"Leave me alone. Buzz off!"

"Ah. Lippy, too. Go ahead, live dangerously."

"Oooh, now I'm really scared."

"Yeah, well, you should be."

And then they'd knock my backpack off the table. Or my water bottle. So that sticky lemonade spilled all over the floor.

"Dumbass!"

"What? Say that again!"

"You dumbass!"

Of course they didn't care for that. They'd rip up my papers when I was in the bathroom. When I got back there'd be nothing left. My notebooks would surface days later. I'd find notes in my backpack with "Asshole" written on them.

I missed Dani. She seemed so far away in my old classroom, one floor up and two corridors away.

∽

"So how's life going in your shack of a rowhouse?" Sulzer asked cheerfully, as he walked beside me chomping on a piece of gum.

We were on our annual fall hike and had been struggling up a mountain for hours. At the top there was supposed to be some kind of cabin where we were going to spend the night. Probably Mr. Berger was lost for the three-thousandth time and we would never get there.

I sighed when I thought about the blisters on my feet and the bandaids that I didn't have with me.

At last we took a break.

Berger waved his arms around and beamed.

"Isn't this beautiful? Isn't it absolutely fantastic? This air! This light!

My feet were killing me.

He looked around at us lying there dead at his feet and shook his head.

"What sad shape you're in. No conditioning, no backbone, no nothing!"

Then he looked at Sulzer, who was looking pretty fit compared to the rest of us, kibitzing around and making stupid jokes.

"Look at you, man, leaping around like a young buck! Didn't think you had it in you."

Sulzer laughed and stuck his hands in the pockets of his Burton windbreaker. "Hey, for a two-fisted drinker like me, a climb like this is nothing."

Berger frowned, opened his mouth to say something, but Sulzer interrupted. "It was a joke, professor, a little joke. Don't you have a sense of humor?"

The teacher gave in. "Don't push it, Sulzer!"

His warning tone told me that he would probably crack the whip over us even more now to pay Sulzer back. You idiot, I thought, not knowing which of the two I was referring to.

I let myself fall to the back of the pack. There was no one I could talk to anyway. But then suddenly Sulzer was right beside me, offering me a stick of gum and asking how things were going in my shack of a rowhouse.

I looked at him, tried to get mad, but I didn't have the energy for it.

"My grandmother would kill you for calling it that!" I said.

He grinned, and I wondered whether there would ever be a situation that would wipe that grin off his face.

"Well," he said. "She'll never know. Do you want me to carry your backpack?"

I was so surprised that I stopped walking, and before I could say anything, he had taken the pack, which had been hanging off my back like a hundred-pound boulder, and slung it over his own shoulder.

"Come on! We don't want to lose the others. We're probably almost there, and you can rest."

"How come you're so fit?"

"I like going into the mountains. It's probably the only thing Berger and I have in common."

"You've done this a lot?"

"I used to go almost every weekend. With my parents. They were freaks." He laughed quietly, kicked a stone on the path.

"Used to? You don't anymore?"

He shook his head. "Now they're just into making money, and if they have any time they go off on their own 'self-discovery' trips." He grinned again. "But at least we don't live in a shack."

I had to laugh, even though I didn't want to. I barged after him and he raced ahead and I followed panting behind him. And eventually the hut came in sight.

In the evening we sat around a campfire and cooked our little sausages over the embers. The sun had gone down behind the mountains, and it threw its last rays into the clouds so that they lit up like fireballs, red and orange and gold. We watched and watched and it was so beautiful and then the light was like angel hair and then it dissolved into dusk.

Sulzer sat next to me and on his other side, half hidden by the flames, sat Vanessa, Yvonne and Sandra, the bitch witches as he called them. They whispered and giggled and cackled, looking over at us the whole time.

"Just ignore them," he said, when he saw me glancing at them. "Or isn't that possible?"

I shrugged. "Don't know. Not always."

Slowly it grew dark, the fire died down, the last embers blinked.

"Okay," said Berger. "Time to sleep. It's late. Get out your sleeping bags and tuck up. We've got an early start tomorrow."

A few kids grumbled, but only out of principle, because basically we were all tired as dogs.

Before Sulzer and I turned in, we threw a last look out the window. That's when we saw Berger snuggling up to the French teacher. The worst-kept secret at school was that they were lovers.

Sulzer nudged me and grinned.

◌

When I flunked my French test, I grabbed my bike, rode over to our house, stood in front of it and stared at the garden.

It's your fault, I thought, but I knew that was bullshit, that it was your fault, my elm tree, because you were so, so far away.

I felt a sob, an ache. It was still my wishing tree, and it should have stopped all this from happening, having to leave our house and our garden. And it had blown it!

Suddenly I was shocked to see the front door open, and before I could run, there was Mrs. Springer.

"You're Charlotte, aren't you? Charlotte Seibold."

"Yes, I am," I said, and felt anger in my heart. "And this is our house."

"Hm," she said. "Hm. Yes. It *was* your house, I know that. Until your father sold it to us."

You bitch, I thought. You bloody bitch. And I gave her my death stare.

She seemed not to notice, stayed all friendly. "Would you like to come in? Look at your old room?"

And that's when I took off. Did she take me for an idiot, or what?

Maybe she'd put a pink couch in there, one with ribbons and frills, perfect for Sophie, for her bloody little pink-loving Sophiekins! I was supposed to look at that?

My classy suit of a father had sold the house without even asking us first. Mum said he had to do it because he needed money for his bimbo, and he had to pay for us, too, and supporting three kids wasn't exactly chicken feed.

The house was where he grew up. Me, too. After Nana died, Granddad moved into a seniors' home and the house was empty.

"Why don't you move into it?" Granddad asked. "It will soon be yours anyway, and it will just fall into disrepair if it stays empty."

So he gave us the house and we moved in. And Mum had Oliver, the screaming little brat, and night after night Dad would go, "Thank God. At least here in the middle of nowhere no one can hear him. The kid can scream his head off if he wants. In the city they would have thrown us out long ago."

My parents got busy fixing it up. We spent hours in tile shops and at IKEA and garden centers and that's how it became my house.

I dug up heaps of dirt that later became a patio, and picked the colors for my room myself, so that in the mornings when the sun came into my yellow room and shone on my bed, I knew it would feel at home.

Granddad never got the house back. He forgot his old life. Each day a little more. The house, and us, and the world.

They called his forgetting Alzheimer's.

Yeah, so that's the story with our house. I loved it and I never wanted to leave or give it up. But Dad …

We put a pattern of tiles around the window of my room, so it was the nicest one in the whole house. It had a gable and a balcony and in the garden outside stood my elm tree.

Every evening I would lean out over the railing to get close to it. I felt its leaves, its greenness, I'd whisper to it out there.

Will you miss me, I asked before we left, and I think I saw it nod.

I know. A tree doesn't miss anyone anywhere any time, but maybe … my elm was different. More like a pet. Kind of like a cat or, I don't know. It was just my special tree.

"It's not forever," Mum said, when we crawled away to Grandma's. "We're just in transition until we find something in the country. We'll make it really nice, put red, orange and yellow tiles around your window again just like before. What do you think, Charlotte?"

I nodded. "Sure, Mum, let's do that."

But I knew better.

∽

Dad said so, too, that it was no big deal. He said it wasn't true that he didn't like Mum anymore, that I mustn't misunderstand, that it was just that he and Mum didn't want to live together anymore, couldn't live together anymore. And did I understand that. That it was important to him that I understood. Really.

"Do you understand that? Charlotte?"

I shrugged. He sat across from me, real casual, stirring his coffee and waving at the waitress so he could order some cake.

I sipped my soda, bored. I was supposed to understand everything and not be cranky ever and I should just want the best for my brothers and me.

"Charlotte?"

I didn't look at him. What was I supposed to say? That I was super thrilled to have my nice comfortable life ruined? That sometimes all I wanted was to smash everything to pieces?

They were the grownups, and they didn't understand a single thing and that's why …

That's why I just nodded and smiled and ate my cake and talked about how I was dying of hunger and not dying because I was so mad and who knows, maybe that feeling in my belly was just hunger and not anger and I just didn't recognize it.

∾

Not long after that I ran into Babsi. In the mall. By accident.

I'd just met up with Dani again and we were talking about this stupid computer game that the guys in our school loved. And suddenly, along comes Babsi. She looked so much like a Barbie doll come to life that it gave me a stitch in my side.

Shit, I thought, not this.

We both averted our eyes. She started to rummage around in her purse while she tripped past, and I stared in the window of the computer game store. When she'd gone past us, I turned around.

But she did exactly the same thing, and our eyes met. I don't know who was more horrified. In any case, she made the first move. No wonder. She was the grownup, after all. She nodded at me and even smiled a little. I just stared. She kept going.

Only when she'd gone around the corner and I couldn't see her anymore, did I feel Dani pull on my sleeve, all excited.

"Was that her? Was it?"

"Yeah. That was her."

"Wow! She looks good."

I shook her off, suddenly felt very tired. Like I'd just gone on an endless hike with blisters on my feet.

"Really? Do you think so?"

Dani looked at me, and when she noticed that I noticed that she felt sorry for me, she looked away.

"Well," she said. "Not really. More a bit like Barbie. Way too tarty."

But it wasn't true. Babsi wasn't tarty, she was just good looking. A real beauty, in fact. It was shitty.

I remembered our first official meeting. Dad had picked up me and my brothers and taken us to a pizza place and there she was. Babsi. She just ate a little bit, just a tiny salad, so at least someone was helping Dad save money.

Not us, though. We tucked into whatever was on offer, and then some. Later Oliver wanted a new Game Boy and Felix went on about how horribly boring it was without a TV at home and that I was such a bloody cow for ruining the new one and that we didn't have a replacement yet and what could we do about it and whether Dad might have any ideas.

But he didn't, and so my brothers and I had a burping contest because we were so stuffed and had to redigest all that pizza, soda and noodles. Besides, Felix could burp like a machine gun and he loved to show off in public and we laughed ourselves silly.

Mum would have been bright red with shame, but she wasn't there. Dad was pretty embarrassed, too, but we didn't care.

"So," he said finally out of desperation, kind of begging. "So, Charlotte, do you need anything? Do you want Babsi to take you shopping? Do you need a new pair of jeans? A new jacket? Or shoes? Can she help you pick something out? I'm sure she'd be a help and she'd like that. Isn't that right, Babsi?"

Babsi tried to smile, but she couldn't quite manage it, and when she realized it, she managed to squeak out a little yes.

Poor effort, I thought. Very poor. I raised my eyebrows, pursed my lips and said, "Gross! That's it, I've had it!"

Then I stood up and went to the bathroom and stayed there for a while, and when I got back to the table, Babsi had already left, and Dad was practically beside himself with anger, I could see it in his eyes and his flushed face.

He gave me a hundred bucks and said, "Go shopping by yourself."

"Fine," I said, all superior. "Fine. And the kids? What about the kids?"

Then I pointed to the empty chair. "Where has she gone? Can't she take it? Her nerves are that weak?"

And I threw his money back at him.

෴

"Don't you have a chemistry test next week?"

She was standing in the middle of the room, her hands on her hips. The sun beamed down on her in a blaze of glory.

I tried to drown her out, turned up my MP3 Player a bit.

"Hello, missy! I happen to know you're not deaf!"

She kept jabbing me on the shoulder with her finger.

"What?" I said. "What is it!?"

"Chemistry test!"

"Yes!"

"Well?"

I sighed. "Well what?"

"Don't you think you'd better start studying for it?"

"Yeah, sure."

"So? Are you?"

"Yeah. Sure."

"When?"

"Soon."

"But *when*?"

"Soon, already. There's still time."

"You think so?"

"Yes. Yes, I do."

She sat down on my bed and stared at my back. For a long time. Silently. Until I couldn't stand it anymore.

I turned around.

"Mum! What? What is it!?"

She shrugged. "As if you don't know."

"But I'm getting to it!"

She was starting to lose it. You couldn't see it, but you could feel it.

"Mum! Please!"

She didn't budge.

I stood up and went to her. "Mum!" I said. "Mum, I'm going to do it already!"

Then she finally reacted. She slumped over and put her hands over her face.

"Yes," she murmured. "Yes. Do you believe that?"

Then she grabbed onto me and held me tight and pressed her face against my stomach.

"Oh, Charlotte!" she said. "My Ringlotte. We have really landed in the shit. What a shitstorm. And it's my fault! I should have stopped it!"

"What?" I asked. "Stop what?"

"Everything! Just everything. Babsi. The sneaking around. That he was lying to me. I should have stopped it all. Then things could have stayed the way they were. Then you would have your lives back."

"But," I said, "that's not ..."

"No!" she said. "No, it isn't."

Then she left, went out to the garage, got in the car and drove off.

"Where are you going?" But she couldn't hear me.

I kicked a domino piece across the room, mad. I knew I didn't want to study chemistry. How can you study chemistry when you don't know who your mother is and what she's up to and whether she's doing something insane?

But actually, I trusted her. She wasn't the kind of person who went crazy. She always stayed calm in the end. I take after her, too. And when all's said and done, we would make it. At least that's what I believed. You had to believe it. Who else was going to, if you didn't?

When she got home, she was a bit drunk.

"I saw Melchior," she said, stroking my head. "Imagine that. Melchior!"

I couldn't believe it. Melchior? Rudi? The good-looking guy from next door. The one who knew everything, could take care of everything.

"He can help you out with your chemistry, if you

want," she said. "Math, too. And that strange physics stuff. Would you like that?"

She smiled and staggered around our little house and our hankie-sized garden a bit, and it did her good.

∾

Melchior actually did study with me. He came the next afternoon, sucking up to Grandma, was all Mrs. Langstetter this and Mrs. Langstetter that.

Grandma raised her eyebrows a bit and then sent us into the kitchen to study. She gave us a pitcher of juice and a plate of cake and left us alone.

I spread out my chemistry stuff in front of Melchior and he brightened right up, because he was some kind of chemistry genius. And a math genius and a physics genius, too.

He had a company that did something for the environment, that would get us all off carbon. I'd heard Dad talking about it.

And a couple of years ago the mayor gave him some kind of award, calling him one of the city's most outstanding treasures. Whatever that's supposed to mean. Afterwards we were all invited to his garden, and of course there were a couple of long-legged women there, wearing great outfits and jewelry, and they hovered around Melchior all sweet-talky this and that.

And then Dad said in a pointed voice to Mum, "When you make the kind of money he does, you can get the best-looking women no matter how homely you are."

"Right," said Mum, and she shrugged her shoulders.

Dad looked at her strangely. "Maybe you picked the wrong guy. You'd better watch out."

"But, Max," Mum said. "You're jealous!"

Apparently Dad and Melchior were friends and grew up together. But I didn't really believe it and anyway, so what. The main thing was that I passed this bloody test. And Dr. Melchior was able to cram enough knowledge into me, so that's what I did.

∾

In November we got a new guy in our class.

I was sitting at the bus stop early in the morning when he suddenly appeared and sat down on the bench beside me.

"Hi!" he said. "How are you doing?"

He spoke with a slight accent and I looked up, a bit irritated.

"Where are you from?" I asked, glancing over at him. Wow, I thought. Wow. They were going to flip out at school when they saw him!

"Italy," he said. "But we live here now."

Wow, I thought, for the third time. A prodigy, too. Comes from Italy and speaks perfect German.

"So how come you —"

"My mother's from here. From that very street, in fact." He pointed in the direction of my street. "It's sort of a homecoming." He grinned. "My name's Carlo. What's yours?"

And that's how I met him. One day he was just there.

And in the afternoon when Grandma came home from shopping, she set herself down in the kitchen with a sigh, her heavy shopping bag on her lap, and told Mum about Klara Rettenbacher.

"Klara Rettenbacher," she said. "You have a lot in common. Apparently her husband took off, too."

Mum sniffed with indignation. "Listen. My husband did not take off. *I* left *him*. There's a big difference!" She went over to the sink and rinsed out a water glass. "And anyway," she said. "I'm not interested in making friends with Klara Rettenbacher, so get off my back about it."

∾

"Have you seen the new guy yet?" asked Hanna, practically swooning. "Have you seen him? Is he not super adorable?"

"His name is Carlo!" said Verena, and she rolled her eyes. "And he lives in your neighborhood, Charlotte. Did you know that?"

"Well, I'd have to be a complete idiot not to," I said, trying to look cool.

And then Carlo walked into the classroom and suddenly the blood rushed to my face. But thank God nobody noticed, because they were too busy falling all over Carlo.

Well, not really, but with their eyes.

"Morning," he said, dragging out the "o" like a ribbon of strudel dough.

Behind him stood Mr. Berger, who told him to find a free seat.

"Well," smirked Sulzer. "The class is actually full. Where are all these strays coming from? All year nothing and suddenly they blow in like junk at a yard sale."

He grinned at me and gave me a little poke in the side. Then he frowned.

"How come you've gone all red in the face?" he asked, and I heard the sneer and suspicion in his voice. "Like a bottle of ketchup. You're ketchup!"

Idiot, I thought. Why don't you say it a little louder?

"No, *you're* ketchup, you loser!"

Then Mr. Berger came up and made things even worse.

"Pull yourself together, Sulzer, or you can spend your lunch hour with me, understand?"

Sulzer grinned even wider. "Yes, sir, no problem. I'm not doing anything. I'll leave the kiddies alone."

And then he disappeared in the direction of the bathroom and didn't reappear until the end of the break.

Carlo was looking for a place to sit. Behind and kitty-corner from me was the only spot left. He smiled at me but I didn't smile back.

Now things are getting complicated, I thought. Shit complicated.

Why hadn't I said that he lived near me, Verena wanted to know, and was I trying to keep him to himself, and I said that he didn't live near me, at most he just lived in my area. And she said it was the same difference and why was I being so stupid about it.

Then Hanna barged in. "You don't keep someone like that a secret," she said, gobbling up Carlo with her eyes. "Not something like that. If he's cheesecake then Orlando Bloom looks like sandwich bread."

Hanna has the loveliest way of putting things that just sums it up. Besides, she's usually right, and when I eventually tried to concentrate on math, she nudged me again.

Look! Yvonney's already got a war plan in place."

It was true that Yvonne was busy softening up her future victim with encouraging glances and smiles.

"Do you think he stands a chance?" Hanna said, crinkling up her forehead as she took it all in.

I shrugged. "Probably not. Most of them just let themselves be reeled in."

"Yeah," she said dreamily. "Like a spider. And then she sucks their blood and throws them overboard and the rest of us can pick over what's left."

I giggled, while Hanna pulled a face and stuck her tongue out at Yvonne.

"Aren't you exaggerating a little?"

She shook her head and tried to follow Meier-Wutschnigg, who was writing endless math formulas on the blackboard.

"I never exaggerate," she whispered. "You know that."

Then the bell rang and Yvonne was instantly at Carlo's desk, and he smiled and I could feel her giving him meaningful looks.

Shit, I thought later, as I made my way home alone.

Sulzer, by the way, was also getting weird. He was avoiding me. Acting grumpy and dumb.

∾

And then Dani and I had a blowup.

She'd made friends with Conny, from my old class. For a while I didn't notice, but suddenly she didn't have time for me anymore. Always had a stupid excuse. That she had to study something for school, that she had a biology project due the next day. Too bad. Maybe next time. Unless something came up. Her parents were so unpredictable. "You know how it is, Charlotte!"

But I didn't know. Because then I saw her at the mall. With Conny. They were laughing, having fun.

Not me. Because I was alone. And I had nothing to laugh about.

I went up to them. My heart was thumping. I could feel it in my neck.

"Ah!" I said. "So this is your biology project. What's it on? How Dani and Conny go to the mall? A study of how two dumb geese go shopping?"

She looked at me and went pale.

"Charlotte!" she stuttered. "Charlotte, I … Charlotte, you …"

"Well?" I asked. "What? Charlotte, I! Charlotte, you!" I really wanted to rub her nose in it.

She looked like a fish gasping for air, turned red and then white.

"I don't really owe you anything, though, do I?" she asked, this person who was once my best friend.

And that's the way it is in life. That's the way it always is.

I went home, sat on the bus, slouched down, my earbuds in, felt tears fill my eyes, snot in my nose. Didn't want to see anyone, hear anyone.

And that's when Carlo got on.

Shit, I thought. Bad timing, really bad timing. For him to see me like this. Teary and crying. Him of all people!

I turned away, as if I was looking out the window, tried to wipe my eyes without attracting attention, but of course he saw me.

"Hello!" he said. "Are you on your way home?"

I kept looking out the window, but he didn't give up.

"Hey, cat got your tongue or what?"

That did it. Couldn't someone just be in a bad mood without any fuss? Couldn't someone just be sad and cry their eyes out in peace?

"Get lost. You're bugging me."

He whistled softly through his teeth. "The lady's in a bad mood. Should I be scared?"

I turned away from him. "Piss off! I don't want to talk to you. Take your bullshit somewhere else."

Shit, I thought. Shit! Now he's going to get up and leave, and if I ever had any chance at all, I just blew it.

"Why are you being so weird?" he asked. "Did I do something to you?"

"No!" I answered. "It would have been better if you did!"

He stood up. "Maybe you're just crazy," he said. Then he went to the front door.

I watched him go, felt my lips trembling.

That's just great, I thought. Now I've really scared him off.

∽

Christmas was coming.

On the 23rd it snowed, big wet flakes, but it was clear that the snow wouldn't last.

Dad picked me up from school, and we drove into town, walked around the Christmas market and made bets on who could spot the kitschiest Christmas angel. Then we ate sausage dogs and drank punch. The sky was really deep and dark and the snow turned into rain.

We ducked under the awning of the sausage stand, and Dad put his arm around me and hugged me close and I made myself a bit stiff and he noticed and let me go, and then he said that I had already got taller and that I was probably growing three centimeters a day and how tall did I want to be and how much he was missing.

"I'm missing so much. I get so little time with you," he said, and his voice was sad and I held my breath and didn't say anything.

A drunk staggered past, slurring the words to a Christmas carol.

"Why don't we get together more often?" I asked. "Why don't you ever invite us to your place?"

He looked at me for a long time and sighed. "It's not so simple. It's too soon."

"Because of Babsi?"

"Yes, because of Babsi."

I could feel myself prickle.

"But she knows about us," I said. "She knew that you had kids."

He lowered his head, hesitated. "Yes, I know. But things aren't going that well for her right now. I can't ask too much of her. She …"

He left it at that. And I didn't ask any more.

"Do you want something else?" he asked. "Anything?"

I wanted a glittery red Christmas ball. He laughed, surprised.

"Yes," I said. "They're the only ones that light up."

Later he took me back to Grandma's. I grabbed my pack from the back seat and promised to tell the boys that he would be picking them up the day after tomorrow to go skating.

"You'll be sure to tell them?" He leaned over the passenger seat and looked up at me.

I nodded. "Yes. Got it. Have I forgotten anything so far?" I grinned, and then he grinned and then he got out and came around the car and gave me a big hug and I could smell his aftershave.

"I love you, my big girl," he whispered into my hair.

Then Grandma came out of the house and gave him

a bag of homemade cookies and the boys came running out and for a short time everything around us felt as bright and red as my Christmas ball.

∽

The next days were nothing but rain. Shitty vacation. Shitty holidays.

But then, on New Year's Eve, I ran into Carlo. He had gelled his hair, and it looked kind of dumb.

"Hello!" he said, and for some reason I got the feeling he was happy. "How are you doing?"

"Good!" I said. "What about you?"

He grinned.

"Maybe," I said, "we could …" There was something in his eyes that made me brave.

So that afternoon we went to the skating rink.

∽

Sulzer was sitting on the bench in front of the food truck polishing off a kebab. Alone.

I went over to him. "Hey," I said.

He looked up, was surprised, swallowed, wiped his mouth.

"Hey!" he said. "Wow! You?"

I sat down beside him, so he had to shove over a bit.

"What are you doing here?" I said.

"What you see."

"What else?"

He shrugged. "Whatever. And you?"

"Yeah. Same."

It was kind of funny. I was waiting for him to be all cool but he wasn't.

"Maybe," he said. "Maybe we could like … if you have nothing better to do …"

"Um, sure," I said, and I knew right away that I'd hesitated a second too long. "Yes. Great."

He knew it, too. It was like a curtain came over his eyes and he gave me a sour look. "But you do have something better to do."

"No. It's just that today …" And I thought about Carlo, who was waiting for me at the mall. "But you could …" I added, "come, too."

His eyes were so suspicious that a shiver ran down my spine.

"Come where?"

"We're just going to the mall. The usual."

"Who is *we*?"

Suddenly I could hear my heart beating, and it was weird, but I felt a bit scared.

"Carlo," I said.

He burst out laughing. "Carlo! Of course! Carlo! Who else could it be!"

He jumped up and kicked a rock. It flew a good ten meters and smashed against a tree. It was a good thing no one was in the way. Sulzer just stood there with his back to me, stuffed his hands in his pants pockets.

"See you later," I said, and left.

∽

Melchior was reeling Mum in. Melchior, of all people!

Now the shit hits the fan, I thought. And that I should have studied chemistry on my own and never let him get so close.

"Stay cool," Carlo said. "He can't do anything to you. He can get up your ass, though. It'll last a few weeks and then there'll be someone else. But you need to get used to it. This is the way it's going to be. They need it."

I looked at him, curious.

"Yeah," he said, looking wise and calm. "You're talking to a man with experience. How many guys do you think I've seen come and go with my mother?"

I sighed, could just see it, picturing Klara.

That evening Mum came up when I was in bed. She snuggled up to me and whispered into my neck. That she had come a long way. That she thought she could be happy again. That enough time had passed. Maybe not with Melchior, she whispered. No, probably not, absolutely not, but that for now things were nice with Melchior, with Rudi, that she could accept that I didn't understand, but she wanted me to leave her to it.

She said, "You're my Ringlotte, for ever and ever."

And I leaned into her and left her to it. I knew I had to. And so I did.

∽

Klara Rettenbacher's husband didn't take off on her. Not strictly speaking.

He died on her.

Anyway, Klara Rettenbacher married an Italian and had been living with him in his country for sixteen years, and that's why Carlo's name was Carlo, after his father and grandfather and great-grandfather.

Klara was on holiday, in the south of Italy, the Mezzogiorno, and she got a sexy sunburn and a boyfriend on the side. He noticed her from a distance, and because he knew how tricky the sun could be, he brought a beach umbrella for the two of them to sit under and it's true that he got a pretty good look at her under there.

After that, there was no way Klara was going to come back. No chance of her returning to her old life. She was brave, this Klara, very brave. Stayed in a country that was so new and different.

She stayed for seventeen years and learned a new language from scratch. Got used to wearing sun hats and tops with long thin sleeves. Went to the university. Taught German and Italian. Married Carlo the Third. Gave birth to Carlo the Fourth. *Basta.*

And now he had this idea that he could teach me his second language. Just like that. Kept yakking away at me in Italian, which was somehow kind of sweet, but also exhausting, because he didn't care that I didn't understand anything.

"You don't understand a single word," he said, grinning, when I complained. "*Non capisci un corno.* And we've been practicing for so long! You could at least learn your vocabulary."

I fought back. In his language, of course. "*Sei un disastro!* You're impossible! You bug me! *Una peste!*"

It was a riot. We had fun. *Spasso, divertimento, piacevoli ore, diletto.*

"*Vieni!*" he said. "Come here!" And off he'd go and I'd follow.

On our bikes through the field. It was the first days of spring. The first really sunny days. Eventually we started talking about our fathers.

"I'm so mad at him," he said and turned away from me, and I could tell from his voice that he was mad and sad at the same time, and that I knew how he felt.

"I know how you feel," I said.

He whirled around.

"What?" he cried. "What? You have no idea how I feel! None at all! Your old man just took off. He'll come back when he feels like it. When he dumps her, he'll come back! But mine's dead. The asshole! Dead! And you think you can understand that?"

Later, after he calmed down, he told me everything. After he'd kicked and punched the tree. He showed me a photo, too. His father was a good-looking man. Black hair, dark eyes. Like Carlo.

"You look just like him," I said, because I had to say something to break the silence.

He didn't hear me. "My mother," he said, "took it so hard. After that she wasn't herself, and I know I have to help her." He was quiet for a moment. "But I also know that I can't help her."

Then I put my hand on his back. Very softly. I didn't trust myself to do more.

"It's crazy," he said. "But I wait for him. To come back. Of course I know he's not going to. I'm not an idiot, at least not that much of one. But I wait for him because … I don't know why."

That's when I felt that I … that I had comforted him a bit.

"I'm so sad," he said, "and I don't want to be."

Yes, I thought. I know. I know how that feels.

The other Carlo, the grownup father, met up with a

I DON'T LIVE HERE ANYMORE | 55

tree. At 120 kilometers an hour. And was dead on the spot.

"We'd left the Mezzogiorno a long time before," explained Carlo. "We were living in the north. In Milan."

"The Mezzogiorno," I said. The word flowed softly. "Must have been like a dream there."

"No," he said. "No dream. Nothing like a dream. No one had any work. They all left, went north. Only the old people stayed. But if we'd stayed, too …" He went quiet.

After his father died, his mother became restless. There was nothing to keep her in Italy anymore. So she came back to the rowhouse that her parents had left her, that had stood empty for years in the middle of our neighborhood.

Carlo kept bashing at the tree, and from that moment there was a kind of connection between us.

∽

"Sulzer is looking at you like you're a three-scoop chocolate ice-cream cone. Or like a wounded deer," Hanna said at break and laughed at her metaphor. "I've got to remember that one," she giggled. "Bachmann would be happy to see it on my next German test."

She drank out of her water bottle until it was empty and looked at me with a wrinkled forehead.

"He likes you, too. How do you even do that?"

"What?" I shook my head. "That idiot? You're not serious!"

Hanna shrugged her shoulders. "Whatever."

"And what's with the *too* business?"

She looked at me, and when I saw her raise her left eyebrow, I knew she'd seen through me. I shouldn't have told her about meeting Carlo, how we'd talked about personal stuff.

"You really are a little bitch," she said and went to buy a sandwich.

When she came back, she had a bit of mayonnaise on her upper lip.

"You've got something right there," I said, and smeared the goo across her face.

She freaked out. "Hey! Are you crazy? Just you wait!"

I started to run, down to the ground floor, and she came after me. The principal was standing at the bottom of the stairs, his arms raised.

"Whoa, there, ladies! We do not run in the halls!"

She caught up to me in the bathroom. We were laughing our heads off like a couple of lunatics. When we got back to the classroom, sweaty and exhausted, Yvonne was sitting in Carlo's seat and showing him photos. She was flicking her hair back like a pro.

"So?" she said. "Give up, Charlotte Seibold? You are so finished."

For a second I considered hurling something back at her, but Carlo was lounging on the bench and he grinned, and over in the corner I could see Sulzer chomping on his meat sandwich and he was grinning, too. He looked a little leery, but whatever.

I decided I wasn't too worried about Yvonne.

∾

They were open secrets. That Meier-Wutschnigg was really a biker chick at heart and was into AC/DC.

That was Verena's gossip, anyway.

That Klara Rettenbacher, who'd been teaching German and Italian at our school and who wasn't called Klara Rettenbacher anymore but Frau Klara Giuliani, was the hottest number in the school, as Sulzer put it.

That the principal got totally tongue-tied whenever he caught sight of her.

That someone should give Sulzer a good punch in the mouth one of these days.

Carlo settled that one in the end, and with perfect timing, after Sulzer called his mother a horny old broad, accompanied by a hand gesture that Carlo did not find amusing.

It happened so fast that we were all too astonished to react. Suddenly Sulzer was on the ground spitting blood.

"Shit!" he said, spitting out a piece of something white that looked exactly like his upper left incisor. "Shit, you asshole! Are you crazy?"

Carlo raised his eyebrows, said nothing and marched back to his seat. Not a second too soon, because suddenly the door was ripped open and Berger stormed in. He was on supervisor duty and had probably heard or suspected something. He had a seventh sense for stuff like that.

"Verena, you keep your mouth shut," Sulzer muttered in Verena's direction.

Verena kept quiet and stood still.

"What's going on here?" bellowed Berger. "Can you not be left alone for one minute?"

When he saw Sulzer struggling to his feet, his hand covering his mouth, he sighed.

"Sulzer, not you again. I should have guessed. Is there never any peace with you? What have you done this time?"

"Nothing!" said Sulzer. "Nothing. No panic, sir. Everything's cool. Just bumped into something."

"Bumped into something!" Berger sighed again, looked around at the crowd suspiciously, seemed to consider what to do for a minute, and opted to withdraw. "But from now on the door stays open, is that clear?"

"Yes, sir!" Sulzer clicked his heels together and saluted.

Shaking his head, Berger turned around.

"You're pathetic, Sulzer," he said. "Absolutely pathetic."

"Yes, sir! Boss!"

Sulzer stood there, frozen at attention, until Berger was out of sight. Then he wandered down to the back row, to Carlo, who was frowning.

"So, yeah," Sulzer said. "This is just whacked. The tooth is gone."

Carlo shrugged, said nothing.

"Got any ideas?"

Carlo stood up. "Don't know."

They stood there across from each other, and I thought that now the shit would really hit and that maybe Verena should have snitched after all.

You could cut the air with a knife. It was like a wall of ice.

But then suddenly, Sulzer started to grin.

"Don't shit yourself over it," he said.

"I'm not going to," Carlo said.

"Okay, so we're good."

"No, not good. In future leave my mother out of it."

And Sulzer raised his hands and said, "Got it."

And then they talked about the tooth, and Sulzer said things were already settled and Carlo shouldn't shit himself over it, and Carlo, real cool, answered that he had no intention of shitting himself and that he was from southern Italy after all and Sulzer knew what that meant, and Sulzer, kind of in awe, nodded and said, "Yeah, I get it. *Camorra!* Right!"

If Meier-Wutschnigg hadn't walked in right then, it would have gone on.

In any case, it was the beginning of a friendship. I have no idea how, but it was.

∽

I went shopping with Mum. I needed new jeans and new shoes because somehow everything had got too small and too short on me.

So I tried stuff on like there was no tomorrow, one thing after another, and Mum played along, constantly bringing me new things. It was nice, I liked it, spending time alone with her, something we hardly ever did.

I struggled into the next size, but it was tight, and I began to sweat.

"Mum," I said. "Mum." But she didn't answer. I shoved the curtain of the dressing room a bit to one side and looked out.

She was standing not far away, chatting with someone. She had a smile on her face, but it wasn't a real one. When she saw me she nodded, and the woman she was talking to turned around.

With a pang, I recognized her.

A tiny, blonde puff pastry of a woman. Mrs. Springer. The one who got her claws on our house.

She came over to me and I thought, Shit now I'm stuck, in these too-small pants, in this change room, and in front of her.

"Hello, Charlotte," she said, and her voice was like candy floss, too sweet. "How nice to see you here. Your mother says you're doing your spring shopping."

And as if on cue, in swooped Sophie. She cozied up to her mother and stared at me with her big bright eyes, and I knew that my wishing tree was doomed.

I looked at Mum and thought, Shit, help. Get me out of this! And Mum looked at me and I knew that she would …

"Yes, Mrs. Springer, so … in fact we're in a bit of a hurry, we have to pick up the boys. Are you coming, Charlotte? I'll be at the cash."

And that was that.

In the car we were quiet for a bit and then Mum put her hand on my knee and I thought about the rose-pink in my old gable room that I could no longer imagine myself in anymore.

That night I dreamed about our house and about the Springers. It came floating toward me, a little cream cake with yummy soft cream that said, Yes, don't worry, they would take care of it, look after the house. But I had my doubts and I said that Mr. Springer gave me the creeps, he was such a grouchy old bastard.

In my dream Mrs. Springer looked at me sadly and words fell out of her creaminess, one sentence. "You must have a little faith, just a little faith," she warbled, and she floated away, leaving a trail of luscious cream behind her.

It was just a dream, I thought the next morning, before I walked out into the sunshine. But then I thought, maybe the Springers could do it, even though we couldn't. Maybe they were the ones who would really stay, who wouldn't go down the garbage disposal, wouldn't be eaten up and mown down the way we were.

∾

They came and pulled Sulzer out of class. Right after math period, just like that. The police — not the normal kind in uniform, but ones wearing suits, the more senior guys.

"They're the ones who know what questions to ask," Sulzer said later, clicking his tongue in a knowing way. "Damn, until you're like butter in their hands."

He kept saying "Damn!" It was like his middle name, Erwin *Damn* Sulzer, and he said it like he was spitting off the bridge.

I met him there toward evening. He was hanging over the railing, letting his arms swing, looking weird, somehow, switched off and forgotten. I'd been at Hanna's and I was already late. My mother would be pissed off anyway, so it didn't matter if I was a bit later.

"Hey," I said, getting off my bike.

"Hey," he said and spat into the water, which was calmly flowing more than twenty meters below.

"What was all that about?" I asked.

He turned and looked at me, annoyed. "What was all what about? What are you talking about?"

"You know, at school. Those guys who came ..." I didn't know what else to say, felt awkward.

"What about them?" he said. "What!?"

"Why did they take you with them?"

He laughed, an angry, bright laugh. A weird laugh. A laugh that wanted to smash everything to bits and was almost crying at the same time.

I froze. As suddenly as he'd begun to laugh, he stopped.

"They all want you to go to hell," he said. "Did you know that? Even Hanna, sometimes." He looked at me. Interested, watching, hostile.

"But, I —"

"No, no one but *you*. You've landed yourself a nice little Italian. Do you really think they'll ever forgive you for it?"

I held tight onto the handlebars of my bike, didn't know what to say.

Finally I found my voice again. "And you?"

He looked at me, and I knew I shouldn't have asked. We stared at the water in silence.

"We were fooling around with fire," he said after a while. "Just a bit. It was the dumpster, and so the stuff went up like tinder. Voom!" He laughed quietly. "It was no big deal. The cops are taking it way too seriously."

"Who?" I asked. "Who set the fire? Carlo, too?"

He looked me in the eye quickly.

"Yes," he said with a strange mix of scorn and anger. "Of course that's what you want to know."

I shut up.

"Think about it," he said. "Wouldn't they have dragged him out of class then?"

You jerk, I thought. You're ticking me off.

"So," he said, and he blinked a bit. "No worries. Your sweetie isn't doing anything bad. He's way too well brought up for that."

"You are such an idiot!" I said.

"Yes," he said scornfully. "I know. That's what girls like you always think."

His eyes were clear again, and I was starting to think I had no business being here.

"So I'm going now," I said.

He looked at me coolly, shrugged his shoulders. "Whatever."

But I didn't leave. I just kept standing there and didn't move my bike from the railing.

"No one from school hangs around here," he said. "Don't you know that?"

"So why do you?"

He shrugged. "I don't know. Nothing. It can be good for a laugh and passes the time."

Suddenly this weird sad look came over his face, and I began to realize what I'd basically known all along, that stuff was definitely bugging him.

"Yeah," he went on, chewing on his lower lip. "You know, I don't particularly want to go home."

"Really?" I asked carefully. Somehow I knew he wanted me to ask.

"No," he said slowly. "My old man's been a bit weird lately."

And then his eyes filled up and his upper lip trembled a bit and I thought, Holy, what kind of shit is this?

"They want to get rid of me," he said. "They want to send me to boarding school, to get rid of me, leave them in peace. If I take one wrong step, if I get into any kind of shit again, then they're kicking me out! Then I'll be sent to some kind of school for delinquents."

"So just don't get into trouble," I said. "Is that so hard? Can't you manage it?"

He looked at me thoughtfully. "I have this urge to set fires," he said. "Maybe even set the world on fire." He grinned, and I didn't know whether to take him seriously. "We're the lost ones," he said. "The lost generation."

"Are you nuts?" I said. "Where did you get that crap from?"

He looked at me blankly, then swung himself up onto the bridge railing and balanced on it. Just like that. I couldn't believe it.

Finally he jumped back down with that Erwin Damn Sulzer grin on his face, saw that I was frozen in shock.

"Hey! Chill out. I've practiced this a thousand times!"

I felt this huge anger.

"You idiot!" I hissed, swung up onto my bike and rode off.

"I'm training for the circus!" he cried. "It's my gift to the world! Haven't I told you?"

I gave him the finger. His laughter rang out behind me.

The next morning he was waiting for me by the coat rack.

"I've been thinking," he said. "About your advice. About behaving myself." He grinned. "Maybe I won't join the circus. Maybe I'll become a cop."

∿

We had phys ed first period. The boys out on the field, the girls in the gym.

"They've both got a crush on you," said Hanna, when I told her everything that had happened, and she sighed. "Life isn't fair."

I thought about what Sulzer had said. That the others all wanted me to go to hell.

"Hanna," I said, hesitating.

She turned to me, curious. "Yeah?"

My heart started beating hard. I wanted to ask her whether it was true, whether she was like the others and …

"What?" she asked. "What is it?" Her eyes were very bright behind her glasses, but when she raised her eyebrows, I saw some vague sadness there, and so I ended up saying something completely different.

"Hanna," I said, and swallowed. "Why couldn't the two of you, you and Sulzer, I mean, that it would be great if the four of us, if we could …"

She met my gaze and held it so firm that I thought my heart would stop beating.

"Thanks for the charity," she said. "When I tell Sulzer what you just said, you are a dead woman."

∾

I was sitting on the bus, heading downtown so I could walk around, when suddenly there they were in front of me.

Carlo and Sulzer.

"Hey," they said, and grinned. "What a coincidence. Want to join us?"

I shrugged. "Where to?"

"To the new mall," Carlo said. "On the west side of town. It opened on the weekend."

We went there. Two giant towers stood on either side of the entrance, one row of stores after another, a crazy collection of boutiques, specialty stores, supermarkets, fast-food stands, dollar stores. We zigzagged up and down through the different levels, in the elevators, on foot. Our shoes clacked against the concrete steps on the stairways.

After we'd stopped for a hamburger and fries and milkshakes, and I was starting to think it was getting quite late and that I should get home, Sulzer had his wicked idea.

We were standing in the middle of a grocery store in front of shelves full of shower gels and shampoos and organic chocolate.

Carlo seemed to suspect what was coming. He shook his head in a warning way, but Sulzer's eyes were flashing, and I knew that he had to do whatever was coming next.

"Just one more time," he whispered, and he looked at me and his eyes were all blue and innocent. "Just one more. Okay?"

I was speechless.

Then Sulzer started running his finger along the shelf. Just a finger at first, then his hand and finally his whole arm, right to the back of the shelf. And then the next one and the one after that.

Everything began to move, like a chain of dominoes, everything started to wobble and then began to tumble down. Tubes and jars and soaps and chocolate, makeup, toothpaste, everything rolled and fell, crashed to the floor and shattered, making a huge noise, mess and chaos.

I was practically paralyzed and just stared at Sulzer. He seemed a bit stunned at this huge thing he'd done, even a little taken aback, but more than that I noticed that he felt good. It was like he was drunk on the sensation of all the falling, the bouncing, that he loved the noise and the rage of it, it felt that good.

I felt like he had this laughter inside him, and slowly I felt it inside me, too, and it confused me, this laughter and trembling and a thrilling sort of fear all at the same time. I stood frozen, like I was no longer capable of thinking, just transfixed by the gleam in Sulzer's eyes.

I don't know how long it lasted. Seconds, minutes, I don't know. But finally Carlo pulled me back, grabbed my arm and screamed in my ear that we had to beat it, and fast, didn't matter where, but we had to get out of the capitalist temple right away, before the cops could get a hold of us.

And I also knew, was a thousand percent sure, that Sulzer would never, ever, become one of them.

We ran to the exit as if the devil himself were after us, like we were escaping from hell. I could still hear Sulzer's laughter in my ears and I felt Carlo's hand in mine. We ran for our lives, away from the chaos and the security guards and while we ran, out of the mall, down the street and into the dusk, and while my heart and my lungs were practically breaking out of my chest, I felt Carlo's hand in mine and that he was holding on, holding on tight.

At some point we stopped and leaned against a wall or a tree. We gasped and moaned and spat and groaned, and my tongue hung out of my mouth, loose and dry like the innersole of some orthopedic shoe.

Then I heard Carlo swearing at Sulzer, calling him a bloody asshole.

Sulzer ignored him. He was holding his sides, still roaring with laughter. "Did you see that chick's mouth hanging open? And the guy who tried to sick his dog on me? Who said, "Bello, attack!" He slapped his thigh and killed himself laughing. "Bello! Attack!"

And then suddenly Carlo's anger just evaporated in the air and I caught my breath and then we were laughing, too, and shouting, "Bello! Attack!" We were buckled over and hysterical and completely beside ourselves. "Bello! Attack!"

It was like a kind of hymn, and I knew that after that it would be our code, like a badge or ritual, for the rest of our lives. "Remember that? Bello, attack!"

At some point the fun was over.

"My parents," I said slowly, pulling myself carefully upright. "My parents are going to kill me."

"Whatever!" Sulzer was completely unimpressed. "You can survive more than you think." And he grinned.

Pompous ass. Completely high.

∾

We were worried for the next few days. Whether someone had seen us who knew us. Whether someone would tell. Whether the cops would come back to school and take us away.

But nothing happened.

We brought Hanna in on it and sent her to the scene of the crime. We didn't dare go ourselves, so we waited a safe distance away.

She came back, grinning, said everything had been cleaned up and put back in place. But one of the clerks had followed her up and down the aisles, never letting her out of sight. Obviously the capitalist temple was on juvenile-deliquent watch.

And so suddenly we were a cool gang, Sulzer, Carlo, Hanna and me.

Mostly we hung out at Carlo's place, where we could pretty much do whatever we wanted.

And once we went over to my old house and I showed them my wishing tree.

We were walking through the field. It was Saturday. Snow had fallen overnight, more than we'd had before. Everything was soft and quiet. We tried to make noise as we walked, but it wasn't possible. Sulzer had scrumpled up my hair, just joking, sure, but I didn't like it and I told him to stop and not be such a twit.

"Yikes!" he said. "Twit? I'm a twit?"

We ran around in circles, all over the place, rubbing our hands together to warm ourselves up, but it didn't work.

All at once I had an idea.

I stopped so abruptly that Hanna crashed into the back of me.

"I know!" I cried. "I know what. I want to show you something. Come with me!"

We tromped across the field, laughing and talking the whole way, pelted each other with snow, screeching and shrieking. Everything felt easy and light.

Suddenly my house loomed up in front of us. Bits of mist streaked around it, smoke was coming from the chimney, a couple of windows were lit up. The branches of my elm tree were bent over with icicles and snow, and the new shoots were all frozen, though they looked mostly alive.

We stood there and were very still. Only Sulzer clicked his tongue in an approving way.

"That's it," I said finally. "That's my house."

They stared at it, full of awe. And I knew they thought it was beautiful.

∾

"You little ass-lick," hissed Yvonne, and she swiped all my stuff off my desk with a single sweep of her arm. She'd thrown a glance at Carlo but must have realized that Carlo was looking at me.

And so it was war. Open war. She threw my phone in the toilet.

We ran into each other by chance in the bathroom. She was putting on her eye makeup. She told me not to look at her that way and that there was nothing she could do about the fact that I was so ugly and pathetic.

It was so absurd.

"You must be out of your mind!" I put my phone on the counter while I washed my hands.

She was still dabbing away at her bloody eyelids when she pointed out that with the fat on my hips I could probably feed half of Africa.

I was speechless.

"What have I ever done to you?" I said. "I can't help it if —"

"A loser like you can do nothing to me!" she said coldly.

Then my phone rang. Unfortunately. I could see from the display that it was my father calling, and I went to grab it, but she was faster.

She'd already snatched it up. "Oh, look at that! It's Daddykins! Checking to see whether you made it to school like a good girl. Should I tell him that you skipped out yesterday? And that you're hanging around with the biggest loser in the school? Here, Vanessa, catch!"

Vanessa, who'd just come through the door, reacted quickly as the phone went sailing over my head. It kept ringing, until my father hung up.

You damn asshole, I thought, and then I screamed it in her face. I knew I would have gone off on Yvonne if there had just been the two of us. I'd already smacked her once.

"Better get it," she crowed, grabbing the phone from Vanessa. "Better answer before Daddy gets mad!"

I almost had it, but then she took those deliberate steps into the toilet stall, held the phone over the toilet bowl and …

… let go.

My screams of anger did no good.

"Your own fault," she said. "You were just too slow. You had a fair chance."

Yvonne and Vanessa looked at each other, giggled, then marched out triumphantly, while I leaned over the toilet and fished out my phone.

∿

Melchior was making himself right at home at our place. Not staying overnight or anything but by making himself indispensable. Less charitable people might have said he was sucking up, because before you knew it, suddenly everything Melchior said seemed like a good idea to Grandma.

"Should we have the oil tank filled, Mrs. Langstetter, time to start thinking about autumn! Oh, and by the way, there is a wonderful new exhibit showing at the city museum, maybe we could all go together…? And what do you think about a picnic on the weekend, Mrs. Langstetter, they're forecasting good weather!"

Mum just grinned and shrugged her shoulders.

And then all of a sudden we were talking about a future that had nothing to do with Grandma's rowhouse. In fact, it seemed that Mum was seeing this future in connection with a neighborhood that we were very familiar with.

One day she took me aside and started asking weird questions. Whether I could imagine going back, and what would I say to that? No, not back to our old house, not that. But back to our old neighborhood. It would be so great. Back to the suburb in the country, near the Danube, where we were so happy.

And wouldn't you know that Melchior just happened to have a big house with a huge garden, and he'd asked whether she could imagine moving in with me and the boys ...

And so she was asking me first because I was the oldest.

I looked straight at her and searched for an answer. I got none.

When it got dark, the boys came to my room and I knew that she had talked to them as well. They lay beside me on the bed and asked many questions.

Whether Melchior was going to be our new father, and what did I think of that. Whether they had to call him Dad. Whether they might even have to do what he said, which would be weird because they already had a father. And what did I think of that, moving into his house. And because of course he couldn't move into Grandma's tiny house, which was already too small.

I hardly knew how to answer their questions. Mostly I just shrugged my shoulders.

They lay on either side of me and the three of us stared at the ceiling, and then Felix asked whether maybe the Springers might move out of our house some day so that we could move back in, and that we would *have* to move back in because who else could?

"You're crazy," said Oliver. "The house has been sold, we'll never live there again. Right, Charlotte?"

I gulped. And thought for a long time. And finally said that I couldn't see us ever moving back into our old house, either.

And then Felix started to cry, very softly, like in slow motion, and I didn't know how to comfort him, and neither did Oliver, so we just put him between us and held him tight.

∽

Carlo was homesick. He got like this every April, and it was at its worst around the day his father died. His mother was now involved with the school principal, and that really didn't make things any easier for him. The only comfort was that it probably wouldn't last long, because it never did.

When I got to school one morning, the principal was standing there in the hall looking out the window with a gloomy expression on his face.

"Has the big day come?" I asked Carlo. "Did she send him packing?"

Carlo nodded. "Yes," he said. "Tomorrow's D-Day. Even if you make it this far, this is as long as it lasts before she dumps them."

"How many others have there been?" asked Sulzer, who had just shown up and overheard.

"Don't know," said Carlo. "I've lost track a bit. At some point she'll finish grieving for my dad, and then someone might have a real chance."

He sounded so sad that my heart ached for him.

Sulzer noticed it, too. "And you? Have you finished?"

Carlo shrugged. "Don't know."

We nodded, but didn't dare look at him.

"Sometimes I try to remember what he looked like, and I realize that I don't know anymore, and then I have to go and look at photos of him."

We stood there nibbling on our sandwiches. Outside the sun suddenly broke through and I turned my face to the window, closed my eyes and felt the light through my eyelids.

"Before," Carlo said softly, "I would imagine that something would happen to my mother and that I would be completely alone, with no one. And then I would have to go to a home and live with other kids who also didn't have anyone."

I opened my eyes. We nodded again. We were sitting in the middle of a puddle of sunshine in the hall. It was as if we were sitting in a sea of cotton wool, and the voices of the others were coming to us through cotton.

At the end of the hall Carlo's mother appeared with a bunch of notebooks under her arm and disappeared into the staff room.

"Sometimes," Carlo said, "I ask myself whether they would have stayed together. I mean, you can't take it for granted. Who knows, maybe they would have split up just like your parents, Charlotte."

We were quiet, sat there like we were in this muffled circle of sunlight and then Sulzer of all people said something so cheesy that it made me cry.

"Maybe," he said. "Maybe God especially loves the ones he takes so early, because that way their love is always young."

We just stared at him, and I got choked up hearing someone as cool as Sulzer say something like that about God, and then he got all embarrassed and turned as red as my Christmas ball.

"Of course that's all horseshit," he said. "I read it somewhere. Stop crying!"

"No!" I said and started sniffling again. "Besides, who's crying?"

∾

"Well," Yvonne asked with a sneer. "Are you managing okay? You and the wop? Or do you need some coaching?"

Hanna and I had met Yvonne at a party, she was already a bit smashed, and her new boyfriend, who she was showing off, was obviously embarrassed.

"Thank you," I said. "No need."

She smiled smugly. "Okay, if you're sure. Because my birthday's coming up. I might be in a good mood and feel like doing you a favor."

She reached out and tapped me on the forehead.

You bloody cow, I thought, but I didn't say it.

"Come on," Mario said, pulling Yvonne along. "Why are you wasting your time with all this kindergarten stuff?"

I looked at Hanna, and she looked at me. We grinned as we both thought the same thing. He was a senior, and you had to admit he was cute. His father was a well-known lawyer in town and his mother was a TV host. But … he had a lisp. Most definitely. He pressed his tongue behind his front teeth like a little hamster. That made us happy.

Yvonne chugged down the last of her beer. She was swaying precariously. Mario pulled her sleeve roughly.

"How long are you going to stand here?" he said, swishing his s's.

"I'm coming, sweetie pie," Yvonne said.

Sweetie pie! He was her sweetie pie! What would be next? World peace?

∽

And then came this wedding. We got an invitation.

Karin, Dad's younger sister, was getting married and wanted us to come. Mum hemmed and hawed over whether we should go, guessing that it could be complicated with Dad's huge family, who would of course all show up and be asking questions like "Are you making ends meet with the children, Silvia?" and "Wouldn't it be better to try to talk things out one more time?" and "Was it really worth it?" and "Why didn't you just forgive him?" or other stupid stuff like "Men will be men."

But in the end Mum decided to go, because back in elementary school Karin had been her best friend for many years. That's how she got to know Karin's brother Max, and how he came to be our father.

"Besides," Mum said. "I have nothing to hide."

She wanted to take Melchior, as bodyguard so to speak, and of course us kids. Unfortunately he happened to have a business meeting on the same day, which he couldn't skip. So Grandma came with us.

We barely got to the church on time, and by that point, everyone was already sitting in the pews. We quickly took our places and soon Aunt Karin came down the aisle in her white dress, and she looked like a queen and I couldn't take my eyes off her.

But then suddenly I heard Grandma murmur something that I didn't understand at first. I looked at her, saw that her eyes were glued to something and then she repeated what she'd said.

"Oh, my God!" she muttered again, and I thought, What is it? What's going on?

I followed her eyes and saw my father sitting in the sanctuary, because he was the brother of the bride, and beside him sat Babsi and she had a weird dress on, a very unflattering dress, one that I would never wear because it just made you look fat. Unbelievably fat, so that you looked …

And then I understood.

Shit, I thought. Not this, too.

I looked at Mum carefully, prepared for anything. I saw her face, her chalk-white face and her horrified eyes and that she was trying to make it go away, the paleness of her face and the shock in her eyes and that she was not succeeding.

Dad saw us, too, and I could see he was embarrassed, and I still remember what I was thinking. Why are you so embarrassed, you ass? Because Mum's had such a shock or because of Babsi's belly or maybe both, or maybe even because you said nothing to us, you coward asshole. You said nothing!

When the vows were over at last, we stood outside in the middle of all the well-wishers, ignored the sheepish glances of the relatives, finally delivered our gift, congratulated the happy couple and got ready to bolt when suddenly he stood in front of us.

Thankfully he was alone. No Babsi, no belly.

At first no one said a word. Mum stared into his face and I thought, now she's going to attack him and if it gets too bad, we might even have to rescue him. I felt the way Felix shoved his hand in mine and so we stood there — Oliver, Felix and I — and waited for the drama.

Grandma tried to calm things down.

"Not here," she begged under her breath, and Mum was about to go when Dad found his voice again.

"Silvia!" he said. "Silvia, wait!"

"For what?" she asked, her voice like ice. "Got any other surprises in store?"

He blinked the exasperation out of his eyes for a moment.

"No," he said. "Of course not. I'm sorry! If I'd known you were coming, then …"

"Then what?"

He said nothing.

"You only had to ask your sister," she said.

He just nodded.

She turned to go, with us behind her. His voice followed us. "Come with us to the restaurant!"

"No," Mum said, without turning around again. "Absolutely not. Not in this lifetime."

It was a bit melodramatic, I admit, but for some reason it fit the occasion, and I remember thinking, "You go, Mum! Give it to him! Punch him in the face!"

"But, Silvia!" said Dad, following her. "Please! Don't be a spoilsport. The whole family is here. What am I supposed to tell them? Aunt Hanni is going to want to know the whole story, and she's an old woman. And you were always her favorite."

"I don't care!" said Mum. "I am so far from caring, you can not even believe it."

"I'm taking Babsi home anyway," he said. "This is too stressful for her."

She stood still. "Oh," she said, and smiled ironically. "And you think we can put in a family appearance."

He gave up. Saw that he had no chance. Still, he tried one more time. "The kids," he said. "At least let the kids stay."

"No," she said. "Not on your life."

∾

She drove home like a maniac, screeching the car around the bends in a scary way. Great, I thought. Just great. At least I would have liked to have a chance to say goodbye to Carlo, and to Hanna and Sulzer.

But we were lucky. We survived.

At one point she stopped. Suddenly just braked to a stop. Then she jumped out of the car. To throw up, until there was only bile left. Grandma held her hair out of her face.

Beside me the boys started to blubber, howling like banshees. Whether Mum was dying and they'd be orphans and have to go to a home. Because Grandma was a million years old and would probably die soon and Dad wasn't there anymore and I was too young and what would happen to them.

Suddenly I snapped and I screamed and bawled them out and they shrank back like scared little mice. That they were complete idiots and had always been idiots and they should shut the hell up once and for all.

They were scared stiff and fell silent and I jumped out of the car and went to Mum and yelled at her. That she had to stop. Finally. That I couldn't take all the drama anymore. That she wasn't the only one Dad had shot in the heart.

When Grandma grabbed my arm, I came to.

"That's enough, Charlotte!" she said, and her voice was unusually sharp. "That's enough, now."

We drove home. Mum didn't say a thing. I was worried.

∾

The next day Dad came over with flowers. Mum took them and shoved them in the garbage.

"What do you want?" she asked.

"To apologize," he said, looking down at the flowers. "But it's hard when you behave like this."

Her laugh rang through the room.

"When I behave like this?" she cried. "Me? That's rich! You bring along this woman looking like she's swallowed a cannonball, and you criticize my behavior?!"

Grandma came and tried to calm things down, act as peacekeeper, but it was pointless. Finally she sent him home, because they were getting nowhere.

But when he was almost outside, Mum dealt the final blow.

"We're moving," she said. "Soon. Just so you know. We're moving to Rudi's."

He stopped short. I thought my heart would stop beating.

He turned around.

"What?" His voice was flat, completely clueless. "Rudi who?"

She'd scored. "Rudi who? You know that many Rudis? I don't. I just know one. And we are moving in with him. With Rudi Melchior."

He just stood there, frozen.

"Good one," he said finally. "Really. Good joke. Never laughed so hard."

"No," she said. "No joke. Absolutely not a joke."

He left, and I ran after him, but he didn't see me. He got into his car and drove away.

I lay in bed and cried my eyes out, buckets full, but it did no good. Adults are so stupid, I thought, but that didn't help. In the end, I thought, Love is so simple. No big deal. It just depends on who happens to be around and losers get the leftovers.

And at some point I fell asleep.

∾

"Carlo's here," Mum said, coming into my room and stroking my forehead. I'd caught the flu. Now, of all times, just when it was getting warm. And because Carlo only lived three houses away, he brought my homework over.

"Well?" he said after Mum had left, and he pulled a chair up to my bed.

"Well?" I said back.

He grinned. "I think you'll live."

"How do you know?"

He shrugged. "Manly intuition. Which also tells me, by the way, that you need to take a shower." He wrinkled his nose up a little, and I threw a pillow at him.

Later he told me about school and Sulzer's latest cockup and that Berger had almost had it with him.

We laughed and I felt better and Carlo went to the window and opened it and let warm air in and I leaned back on my pillows and closed my eyes and breathed in deeply.

Then I heard his voice. "Are you sleeping, Charlotte?" and I wanted to open my eyes, but then ... I could feel that he was very close and that he was looking at me and his voice became very soft like the apple blossoms that were blooming everywhere now and I thought, Yes, I'll just sleep. Just let me sleep a bit, my Carlo.

When I heard the door close softly, I opened my eyes and realized my heart was beating madly.

My Carlo. That's what I'd thought. *My Carlo.* I whispered it again, testing it out, and it felt good, but I was startled. I imagined his eyes and knew I could pick them out from a thousand shades, and I could feel the coolness of his skin on my fingertips.

But then I thought of my parents and our misery, and I thought, You stupid cow. Stupid, stupid cow. You're going to lose everything! You're done for! Stuck between a rock and a hard place. Life or death.

Wow! I thought. Holy dramatic. Like an epic poem or something.

And I knew that it would be what it would be, in the end.

∾

So we moved back to our old neighborhood.

Everything was all set up, we each got our own room and were allowed to arrange it the way we wanted. We kids had our own bathroom and every week a cleaning woman came and got rid of all our dirt. It was pure luxury.

However, not everything was that simple. Grandma cried a bit, and you couldn't really tell whether she was sad because we were leaving, or relieved that we finally were leaving. All day she'd been coming out with things like "Don't you think you're rushing into this a bit, Silvia?" and "Aren't you asking a lot of the children?" and "Don't you think you're doing all this now because Babsi —"

But she didn't finish that last sentence, because Mum started to shake and looked like she was going to blow, so it was better for Grandma to shut up or else.

I was also not that sure whether moving under these complicated circumstances would go well, but the thought of more space let alone the chance to be able to look out at my elm tree again cheered me up, and it didn't all seem so bad.

Mum strolled through the house and garden like a countess, a queen, even. Practically floating.

"We're back," she said, and she almost looked awe-struck. "My God, we're really back."

We stood at the window and looked over at our old house on the other side of the hedge. Slowly night fell over my tree as it rose up into the red sky, proud but lonely.

I felt like we would be spending a lot of time standing here by the window and looking over the hedge and remembering and feeling stuff about the past, and I didn't know if that would be such a good thing. Mum must have been thinking the same thing right then because she put her arm around me and it was somehow okay.

Later in the afternoon we met the Springers. By accident. He looked at us like we were ghosts, and she just shook her head.

"Well, look at this! What a surprise!"

In the afternoon Hanna, Carlo and Sulzer came over. Their jaws dropped at how swish the house was.

"Holy shit!" said Sulzer reverently. "This is what I call moving up in the world. This is a palace. Hopefully you can keep it for a while. At least until the summer holidays."

He had just seen the pool.

∾

Dad was a long time coming. He had even been out of touch with Oliver and Felix. Finally he had his third son and could start up again. The rugrat's name was Julian, and Dad came by himself to tell us the news.

Mum wasn't home, which I considered a stroke of luck, and Melchior answered the door. Then Dad was standing in the living room and he looked exhausted and wrecked, but he beamed at us and seemed happy.

"Come on, Max," said Melchior. "Let's have a beer. Are you hungry?"

He was, and I made him toast and eggs and we toasted the new baby and he made us promise to come and see him soon. And it seemed as if we were finally pulling our lives together.

∾

I did go to see the rugrat, just marched over there, didn't call first, thought, I am his sister, after all.

Babsi was quite surprised.

"Your father isn't here," she said. "And I don't know when he'll be home. He's still at the office."

"Doesn't matter," I said. "That's okay. I just wanted to have a look at the kid. I won't stay long."

"His name is Julian," she said, and kept standing in the doorway, probably trying to decide whether she could get rid of me.

"I know," I said. "One of the kids in my class is named Julian. He's a real asshole."

She tried to grin but couldn't quite manage it.

"Oh!" she said.

She let me in, for better or for worse, even offered me a cup of tea. Fennel tea. I said no thanks.

"So, no tea, then," she said, shrugging her shoulders, and she began to feed the kid. "Would you like something else?"

"No."

The brat was sweet, as far as brats go, but he was probably screwed in the end. She unplugged him from her breast and he began to scream. She took him and rocked him in her arms while she walked him around the room.

She wasn't a Barbie anymore. She had no makeup on, she was getting a zit on her chin, and the brat had thrown up on her T-shirt.

I left. I went to my father's office. Walked past his new assistant, who just watched me go by, her mouth open.

He was at least as surprised as she was, but he nodded in her direction to say that everything was okay as he closed the door behind us.

I flopped on the couch that he'd put in his office, and he came over and stroked my hair.

"What's the matter?"

"I saw your son," I told him.

"Oh!" he said, surprised. "I think that's fantastic." And he smiled. And looked a bit tired.

There was a knock on the door. The assistant stuck her head in, looked at him questioningly.

"Not now," he said. "Fifteen minutes."

She nodded and closed the door so softly, you could barely hear it. That's how I knew this was the right time. It was now or never.

So I asked him. Whether he was happy. Now.

If he was surprised, he didn't show it.

He looked at me for a long time, then he sighed a bit. "Oh, my big girl. What do you want to hear?"

And I lost it. I finally lost it. But in a reasonable way. Whether it had been worth it, I hissed. That I wanted to know whether it had been damn worth it, abandoning us!

"Worth it!" he said. "What are you talking about?" He came over to me, put his arm around me. "I know," he said, "that you can't understand it all. Maybe later you will. For sure. Later, when you're grown up and you have children of your own and …"

I didn't listen to any more. The usual when-you're-grown-up shit. I stood up. He kept talking. I'd heard it all too often.

When I was back on the street, I looked up at his office window and shook my head for a long time.

So they still aren't even happy, I thought. No snappy comeback. None of this "Yeah, sure. Everything's just super!"

I left.

∾

It was Sulzer's birthday. We drank beer, and I thought it was disgusting, but Sulzer said you just had to get used to it.

In the afternoon we wandered around town, hot for June, up and down the streets, then to the movies, then to Pizza King, then to Sulzer's place. He could do what he liked there — his parents had gone wherever.

He'd invited us all the week before and because it would mean staying overnight, he went to the trouble to come home with me to ask whether I could go, and he was so polite and nice and harmless, explaining how Hanna was allowed to come, too, and of course Carlo, so it would be our regular group, that Mum was completely taken in.

"Of course," she said. "Your grades have been fairly good lately. Besides, we know you pretty well by now, don't we, Erwin?"

And Erwin Damn Sulzer nodded and beamed at her.

There were a lot of us, half the class and a couple of older ones. We played the Red Hot Chili Peppers nonstop, watched videos with beer and pizza and chips and cake.

But then I suddenly felt like I was going to puke, and I jumped up like the devil was on my back. I ran through the garden into the street, and then that was it. Huge throw-up. Smashed out of my skull.

"Happens to everyone," said Carlo, who had come after me. He put his arm around my waist, held my hair back off my face.

I began to shiver.

"Sit down," he said. "Come on, I've got you. Lean against me."

So that's what we did. He sat on the garden wall and I leaned against his legs, my back against his stomach, his face in my hair, on my shoulder, sometimes on my cheek. I could smell his breath, a crazy mix of beer and pizza and cigarettes.

"I'm drunk, too," he said. "But I can hold it a bit better than you."

Then he began to sing, very quiet and croaky, probably a lullaby from when he was a kid, and I couldn't understand a word and had this terrible urge to laugh and felt my head lying heavily against his neck and I suddenly wanted to nibble it, just a bit —

"Hey!" he said, jumping, and I laughed.

"You taste like salt. Can I do it just one more time? Please?"

He grunted and gave me back his neck and I licked it here and there with the tip of my tongue, and it tickled him and we laughed and rolled away from the wall into the field that was already damp with dew, and we were probably lying in the middle of snail slime but maybe not, and I felt good.

At some point he took me back into the house, my Carlo, and I was amazed. About us and that we were a couple, even when it was mostly three or four of us. Even if I was still drunk.

Later I nibbled on his neck again and then I slept a bit and he said, "You snore. Like an artillery tank!"

"I do not. No way. But you do!"

And then I heard him in my sleep, and it wasn't a dream. I could hear his fingers on my shoulder, stroking my hair and my part and my forehead, calming me.

"You see," he whispered, and I heard him. "You see, you see …"

∾

"Holy shit!" said Sulzer. "Look at you. And where is …" He paused. "Loverboy?"

I knew he was trying to sound sarcastic, like always, but he couldn't manage it. His voice cracked, sounded a bit hoarse.

"Loverboy?" I shook my head. "I don't have a lover."

He laughed, but it didn't sound genuine.

"No? Really? So what was with all that hot making out? Do you think I'm blind? Didn't see you having a good time in my bed?"

"Oh, piss off!"

He raised his hands. "Fine. Fine, already. I won't say another word."

His eyes flinched a little, then he turned and ran his hands through his hair.

"Listen," he said. "I …"

I waited, but he didn't say anything else.

"I have to go home," I said. "Have a shower. Or do you need us to clean up?"

He shook his head, looked at me in a weird way, such a mix of anger and tears that my heart started to beat hard.

"Are we still friends?" I asked.

He laughed shortly. "Friends! Yeah, sure."

Shit, I thought. Then, on impulse, I gave him a hug. He was surprised, I could tell, but then he held me tight. He had already showered and he smelled good, and I could feel him tremble a bit.

"What is it?" I asked, even though I knew. "What's the matter?"

He shook his head firmly, let go of me, stepped back. "Forget it! It's nothing!"

"I'm sorry," I lowered my head, hid behind my hair. "I'm sorry."

"I know," he said. "I know, already. It's okay. No worries. You can't do anything about it." He looked at me blankly. "I never really thought that you … and I … I mean, next to Carlo a mere mortal doesn't stand a chance."

"Don't talk garbage," I said. "It's no big deal. We were both drunk, completely shitfaced, the beer messed with my head!"

He grinned, and it was almost like he was the grown-up. "Yes, that was obvious."

I grinned back, relieved. For a minute there I thought I would lose him.

"Really? Was it that bad?"

"Well, yeah," he said. "You know how things go sometimes. Not exactly pretty." He made a face.

We both laughed and didn't say anything else. We sat on an empty beer case in the garden and drank cola and somehow were self-conscious. About the thing with Carlo. About the thing with us. About everything.

∽

On the way home it began to drizzle, and it did me good, cleared my head. I rode through the field and along the Danube. The sky was bluey-gray, cloudy. But in the distance the sun shone through a bit and made the water sparkle.

Melchior took one look at me and was horrified.

"Wow!" he said. "That must have been some party. Maybe you should head straight for the shower."

I nodded and walked past him to the bathroom. The

shower felt good, and I could just picture Carlo again, how he had turned and brought his face close to mine. How I woke up and was so surprised to see his face so close to me. How I flinched and slipped out slowly so I wouldn't wake him. He slept like a baby, like a prince. Prince Dark Eyes, Prince Soft Mouth, and now ...

"Carlo is here! Can you hurry up?" Mum stuck her head in the bathroom. I whirled around, startled.

She laughed. "Well, hello. That's quite a reaction."

I hurried to pull my clothes together and stuffed them in the washing machine. I turned off the water, she handed me a bath towel, and as I wrapped myself up in it, she hugged me tight, rubbed my back and whispered in my ear, "So, my Ringlotte, are you madly in love?"

And that's when I first knew it, what I had only felt up until now, and I let myself fall into her arms a bit and said, "Yes."

When I went out to the garden, Carlo was standing by the fence and looking up into the branches of my wishing tree. I went over to him.

"Hey!" he said.

"Hey," I said.

"Nice tree," he said.

"Yes," I said.

It was weird. Not like before.

Then we headed out. Into the field. In the direction of the Danube. We were a bit on guard, we walked with a half meter between us. Carlo kept lifting his head and grinning over at me but only every now and then, only sometimes and then really quickly, and between times he would whistle softly through his teeth.

He'd never done that before. It was something new.

Finally we came to the water. We took off our shoes and socks and the Danube sloshed around our feet.

"Yikes!" I said. "It's cold!"

But Carlo went all big man and said, "What are you talking about, you wimp!"

But he didn't say it in a mean way, he said it kind of proud and strong and not to put me down and I could let it go, the wimp thing, because it was somehow sweet and proud at the same time.

"I've never been here like this before," I said. "Not by myself."

"But you're not by yourself."

"No, I'm not." And I looked into his eyes and smiled. They were dark and soft.

I heard him breathe, in and out. I saw the fine hairs on his skin and then … there was the electric feeling of his arm against mine, so soft, so quick. Like electricity.

"This is what I've wanted for a long time," he said. "To be close to you like this."

"And now you are."

"Yes, now I am." And he smiled into my eyes. And I felt proud and happy.

I thought it would be nice to feel his hand on my face, and I didn't know whether he felt it or guessed, because he gave me his hand and I brought it to my face and it was soft and cool.

He smiled, and it felt safe and free, as if there was just the two of us and his hand was on my face and then …

… then …

… he kissed me.

His tongue was sharp at first and then soft and at first I was a bit scared, that oh, God, there was too much spit in my mouth, oh, God, it would gross him out, but then it was okay and he wasn't grossed out and it was …

… it was …

… like come hell or high water, do or die, life or death …

… but sweet in my body and way, way more than that.

And so, I thought. This is it.

And I gave in. To him and me and love. I jumped right in, deep and wide. And I wasn't afraid.

It was like flying. I wasn't afraid.

∽

The bird was lying on its back, its feet pointing up to the sky, its claws wiry and silver, its beak sharp and empty. We found it on the way back. It was very dead. We stopped and looked at it for a moment.

"Let's bury it," said Carlo.

We carried it carefully over to the edge of the path, dug out a little grave with a dead branch, put it in, covered it with earth and leaves. I felt a bit like crying.

"Hmmm," said Carlo. "Tastes salty."

The sky had gone heavy again. Then it started to rain hard and it splashed down, and we ran like the dickens through the warm rain.

My mother stood at the front door and waved us in. Melchior had baked a cake and made coffee, and the smell of it drifted through the house. Our wet clothes clung to us and something new, too, something … exciting.

And summer had finally come.

∾

Super Mario dumped Yvonne. Cold as ice, just like that. We found out from Hanna's sister, who was in his class. He met someone new, and that was it for Yvonne. Contrary to expectations she handled it well, didn't let anything show, was as snippy and mean and as much of a bitch as ever.

"Get out of my way," she groused at me when we saw

each other on the bus in the morning. "You're ruining my day."

I shrugged. "It's a free country," I said, all chummy. "Or didn't you know that?"

She looked like she wanted to stab me in the eye. There was a free seat beside her. I sat in it.

At lunch I met her in the bathroom. I came in and there she was with her face all teary and her mascara smeared. She froze when she saw me. We were both horrified that I'd seen her like this.

She quickly wiped her eyes, tried to walk by me to escape.

Suddenly I felt like I wanted to say something, because we were both girls and we were used to heartache.

"The thing with Mario," I said. "I heard."

She nodded and I saw her pull herself together.

"Yes, I can just imagine. Have you already had your fill of gossip, you and the other idiots?"

"Yes," I said. "Of course. You would have done the same thing."

Her eyes flickered, and for a split second I thought she was going to come at me, but suddenly the corners of her mouth went up and something like a smile lit up her face.

"Yes," she said. "You're right. I would have done the same thing. So it's one-nothing for you."

I had to grin.

She turned to the mirror again and her smile fell. "My God! I look like shit!"

I nodded. "When you're right, you're right."

We both grinned into the mirror and sighed, and suddenly we were standing very close.

Then she fixed her eye makeup and her lipstick so that no one would notice her tears and see how sad she was, and then she left, as proud and arrogant as ever, but before that we winked at each other, and I said I'd always thought Mario was a real asshole and she said she'd already suspected as much, too.

"Bye, Seibold!" she said.

"Bye, Radhauser!" I said. "Keep your head up!"

She nodded and then she was gone.

For a minute I thought about the thing with my phone, but it was such a long time ago and now I'd seen into her heart. But I knew we would never be friends. Once a bitch always a bitch. It was what it was and could stay that way.

∽

Far enough away from the train station, where the tracks cut through the countryside, the four of us lay in wait for the Good Luck Express.

The trains blew their whistles at regular intervals and thundered over our five-cent coins. Sometimes they got dislodged and we found them lying some-where nearby. Mostly they were flat, though, which meant good luck.

We lay in the field chewing on blades of grass and looking up at the sky. If you closed your eyes a bit, it was like it was glazed with sugar, and the trains were riding through cotton and they whistled, but it came out all muffled, not clanking.

The sun clanged, though, if you looked straight at it. It shrilled, like a mighty siren, and we laughed it down and ran in the fields and couldn't reach it through the shimmering trees.

"I'm going soon," said Carlo. "As soon as the holidays start, I'm off. Going south and staying there until the end of the summer. I promised my nonna. She needs me, you know. She's got no one else left."

We were at the Danube. If you walked over the pebbles in your bare feet, they pricked your soles. The sand was hot, the water cold. Kids were screeching and shouting, dug themselves into the wet sand and came out looking like gigantic black slime monsters.

"Yes," I said. "I know. But you're coming back, right?"

He smiled and twisted knots in my hair.

Behind us Sulzer came to a stop.

"Let's go! Last one in's a rotten egg! Come on, Carlo, you lazy bugger!"

They screamed their heads off because the water was so cold. Hanna and I just shook our heads, gave them the finger, laughed.

"You're behaving like seven-year-olds!" cried Hanna. "No, like kindergartners! No, like babies!"

So they came out and grabbed us and pulled us into the water. We screamed bloody murder. It was all so easy, so lovely. So light.

Later Hanna and I covered our feet with sand while the boys roamed through the woods. And eventually Hanna asked the question. Whether we'd done it yet. Whether I was on the pill. Or something else. And to make sure you were never without. That there was stuff like AIDS and getting pregnant and who knew what else.

I looked at her, my eyes big.

"Are you insane? Are you kidding me?"

She blushed. "Well, then what? What's so …"

I shook my head. "It's only been four weeks. Four. I'm not going to do it so soon."

"But four weeks!" she said. "That's a long time."

"Really?"

"Yes."

We were quiet.

"So?" I asked finally. "Have *you*?"

She giggled, didn't look at me. "A bit."

"How, a bit?"

"Yeah, just a bit."

Weird, I thought, that we were having this conversation. And I wanted to know more. Hear more.

"What's a *bit*?"

"I can't explain it."

"Why not?"

"Because … I thought it would be different."

She drew in the sand with a stick. It was a while before she said anything else.

"It's overrated."

"You think so?"

"Yes. For sure."

And she paused again. And I wondered who it was she'd done it with a bit. And then I remembered.

At Sulzer's party there was a guy. A bit older, two or three years ahead of us in school. He came on to her while I was chugging beer.

"And?" I asked. "Are you still seeing each other? Is there something you haven't told me? Have I missed something?"

She laughed, shook her head, looked sad.

"No, you haven't missed anything. There's nothing to tell. Let's go find the boys."

I nodded and took her arm. I heard her sob just a tiny bit and the sun wiped it away. Sometimes it can do that.

Then we went to find the boys.

∾

It was getting dark by the time Carlo and I got home. It was still hot and we made out like crazy and then we jumped in the pool, and Carlo would go home late but we didn't care.

We'd turned on the pool lights and when we swam in the water they shone through us like an x-ray.

Finally we were frozen through, and we got out of the water, wrapped ourselves in bath towels and warmed each other up.

Then I told Carlo about Hanna being so sad.

And how it seemed like everyone had done it. Except us.

"Should we?" he asked and grinned, embarrassed. "We could."

"No," I said. "We shouldn't. Do we have to?"

He brushed the hair out of my face. I liked it, his hands on my face.

"No," he said. "We don't have to. We can decide any time."

That made me happy.

"Yes," I smiled, and reached for his tongue with my mouth.

Any time. Any time, then.

∾

When vacation came, Carlo and his mother went to Italy, to the Mezzogiorno, and I went with Grandma to the Baltic and while we were there we got a strange call from Mum.

She might need a bit of space, she whispered carefully into the phone, and that maybe it had been a bit too soon, the move into Melchior's.

"What does that mean?" I asked, alarms going off.

She was impatient. "But, Charlotte, I just explained! Listen to me!"

She had found a suitable apartment, centrally located between school, Dad's house, Grandma's and Melchior's place. She came across it more or less by pure coincidence and had to grab it. It was fate! Oliver and Felix had already moved in, Dad knew. And what did I have to say about it.

I didn't want to say anything, I was so taken aback, but then I pulled myself together.

"You can't just do this," I said. "You can't just move every few months. And what about Melchior?"

He was still a good friend, she insisted, and would remain so, no matter what happened.

"And who knows," she warbled. "Maybe we'll be back living with him by Christmas. It's just … can't you understand?"

No. I did not understand. I went out to the sea. The Baltic rolled with white surf and cold streams of water and Grandma made comforting noises, but it made no difference.

When we eventually got home, it was all settled. They picked us up together from the train station, Mum and Melchior. She was nervous, kept pushing the hair back off her face and trying to give me a hug. He wore this stiff smile. I looked at him and sighed. What a chump, I thought, putting up with all this, whatever they dumped on your plate.

Then my mother began to talk. That we would be there soon and they'd be so happy to see my face and what would I like to eat, maybe sauerkraut and bean soup and how it was not really the end of the world.

Melchior got our bags and walked them out to the car. We followed, and the whole time Mum burbled on at me. She was practically vibrating, I could tell.

Someone had to stop her. *I* had to stop her, but I couldn't.

I hated her. And I said nothing. I just gave her the finger.

She freaked out. Right there in front of the car, while Melchior was putting our bags in the trunk.

"I am your mother!" she screamed. "You have no right to criticize me!"

I'm not, I thought, I didn't say a word! And what are you going to do about it? Don't you get anything?

My mother raged on. Why she was always the one who had to pay. Whether we didn't also have a father. And what about him. Whether he was always in the right. And so on.

"Leave it alone, Silvia," said Grandma. "Let's just get home. Everything will get sorted out later on."

"No!" said Mum, planting her hands on her hips. "Why can't she at least take the trouble to open her mouth and have a reasonable conversation with me?" She looked at me defiantly.

Okay, I thought. If that's what you want, that's what you'll get. I closed my eyes and then it was as if the words had a life of their own.

"You bloody cow!" I said. "Leave me alone! You can move into your shitty apartment by yourself!"

I felt everyone gasp, and my heart stopped and my throat closed up and I thought about the bird on the side of the path with its legs sticking up in the air, and how they were as thin as wires and then I felt the slap of her hand on my face.

She smacked me, just like that. I held my breath and felt the burning that slowly spread over my cheek, and I had no idea but I thought I probably would have done the same thing if it had been my daughter saying that to me, even though she should have let it go.

I ran, away from the parking lot. But where to, I thought? Where the hell to?

No one was back yet from the summer. Not Carlo or Hanna or Sulzer.

I thought of my father. Right, I thought triumphantly. I'll go to Dad's. He has to take me in, he can't say no, he's my father. Who else but him would take me?

But he didn't. He said no! Plain and simple. The dumbass. He didn't even have to think it over.

Just said no.

"No, Charlotte, that won't work. It just won't. What are you thinking? The place is far too small. You know that already. You've been here. And Julian is here. He screams constantly and doesn't sleep through the night. And Babsi is at the end of her rope already. And so am I."

I didn't want to listen to him anymore.

"Go home, Charlotte," he said. "Your mother means well. Don't be mad at her. I've seen the new apartment and it's nice, Charlotte, honestly. You have your own room. If you were with us you'd have to sleep in the living room. Can you imagine? And where would you put your stuff?"

I didn't try to understand what he was saying. I turned and ran off, believing he would come after me, hoping he would. But he didn't.

He stood on the doorstep, bent over the railing.

"Here, Charlotte! Buy something nice for yourself!"

In his hand was a hundred. I was worth a lot to him.

What a dork, I thought. But I love you anyway. Have to.
Down in the street I called Mum.

"So where is it?" I asked, and she gave me the address.
It wasn't far. Convenient location, as she said.

She opened the door. I walked past her and just asked, "Where?"

She showed me my room. It was new, white, big, smelled like paint. I closed the door behind me. No tree outside the window.

Another window. Another house.

My throat was tight, my heart clenched.

Love you anyway. Have to.

∽

We talked on the phone and he told me about the sea. How it sounded when the rain splashed on the water.

Plop, plop, plop and then faster and faster, plopplop-plop, and I said, "You're crazy. I've heard the rain hit the water, too, and it doesn't sound like that and the sea is the sea, whether it's the Baltic or the Mediterranean, it's all the same."

He laughed.

"I miss you!" I said.

"I miss you. Come here. Come quick. I miss you."

"It hardly ever rains here," he said, and I could feel him thinking hard.

"Yes," I said. "I believe you. Maybe I'll come anyway."

"Are you okay?" he asked. "Are things okay?"

"They're okay," I said.

∾

I stood by the fence. My elm tree looked at me, rustled its leaves a bit, let me go. My old wishing tree.

"Who are you talking to?"

Shocked, I turned around and there was Melchior. Had I been talking? To whom? To myself? To the tree?

"Rudi!" I said. "You scared me!"

"I saw you from the window," he said, "and thought maybe you'd like to come over."

I thought about it. "Yes. Maybe."

"Come on," he said. "I don't think the Springers appreciate you standing in front of their house."

"*Their* house?"

He nodded, grinned a bit. "Yes, it is now."

We went over and sat in the shade by the pool. I listened. Rain on the water. Not plopplopplop. What crap!

"You're soaked," said Rudi. "Do you want to shower and change? I think you still have a few of your things here."

I shook my head, wanted to talk about Mum.

"Why did she clear off like that? Why didn't you stop her? Things were working out here."

He laughed, a bit embarrassed. "What was I supposed to do? Any suggestions?"

I shrugged. "I don't know! But you must. You're the grownups!"

He nodded vaguely, and finally he told me what happened. She said she had something she had to show him, and then they drove into town and she took him to the apartment. It was empty and white and quiet, and he knew right away where things were heading and what would happen.

"I have to be alone right now," she told him while she packed and tears poured down her face. "Give me some time, Rudi. Give me time. First Max and then you right after. It can't be good. There has to be something in between. Some distance. A break. A time-out." That's how it went.

Rudi stood up and went to the pool. Now it was raining down on him, he was wet right through. It had cooled down a little. I tried to hide my shivering but he saw it anyway.

"Go and shower," he said. "Do me the favor. Otherwise you'll catch a chill."

He pulled me up to the house and sent me to the bathroom. I made the water so hot, I thought I'd dissolve in the steam.

∾

"So?" I asked. "Are you giving up? What do you want to do?"

This was after the shower. The mirror was covered with steam and I was looking at myself through the cloud and couldn't see or hear anything, no lighthouse or foghorn.

Later I perched on the couch in the living room, wrapped in a bathrobe and towels. Rudi had made tea. It was already getting dark.

"So? Are you giving up?"

He took his time answering.

"You know," he said then, "I've had a crush on your mother ever since we were kids. But she only had eyes for Max."

I nodded and thought, yeah, I already knew that and what did it have to do with my question, but he jumped up, full of beans, just like the old Rudi Melchior I'd known my whole life.

"So!" he said. "Time to stop talking about all this sad stuff. Come on, get dressed and I'll drive you home. She's going to be worried about you. Or did you tell her where you were going?"

I shook my head.

"Didn't think so."

We drove away past the Springers' house. I turned around and said goodbye. It was time.

"Ciao!" I said silently. "Ciao. I'm leaving you now. You were a good friend, but I won't be coming back anymore. Look after Rudi a bit. He needs it."

Rudi turned to me. "Everything okay?"

I grinned and gave him a little shove. "Yup, everything's okay."

He grinned back.

"One day," he said, "you'll live here again. I can do it, make her see where she belongs. You'll see. I can do it!"

And I had to smile and shake my head a bit.

"Whoever laughs last, laughs best!" he said.

I giggled. It would sure be nice, I thought, and that I had confidence in him.

But that it no longer had to be that way, not for me.

∽

"Oh, my Ringlotte!" Dad said softly. "My Charlotte Ringlotte. Everything has changed so much. And I know it hasn't been easy."

Babsi had gone with Julian to visit her parents, so he took us to his place for the weekend. Oliver and Felix were still sleeping, stretched comfortably on the big bed in Dad and Babsi's room. I'd been woken by the click of the apartment door, and got up to make coffee.

When Dad got back with fresh buns under his arm, the delicious smell of coffee wafted through the apartment. We sat on the balcony, the sun tickling our bare toes. We sighed, things were good, and I closed my eyes.

Suddenly I could feel him looking at me. I turned around.

"What?"

He smiled, gave me a meaningful look. "Your mother tells me you're in love."

"Arrrgh!" I said, surprised.

"Do you want to talk about it?"

"No!"

I was astonished at how sharp my voice sounded. He smiled, but I saw that his feelings were hurt. Whatever, I thought. That's life.

"So not now," he said.

"Right," I said. "Not now."

The sun seeped away in our silence, disappeared behind a cloud and came out again, strong and glittery. *Don't make such a big deal about it. Throw him a bone,* it said, and I looked up in wonder. *Life is short.*

I turned around warily. My father was sipping his coffee. Had he heard it, too?

"What?"

I shook my head. "Nothing."

We were quiet.

I wanted to. But I couldn't. I kept feeling this barrier that stood between us.

"Mum," I said at last, "said that it had to be this way because you, that is, you no longer …"

And then I started to blubber. Even though everything was so long ago and things were normal now — the big fight, the move, the divorce, the new little brother.

Dad pulled me to him and I clung to him like a wet noodle and I could hear his heart beating, very regular and so loud in my ear, and I thought, he is my father and nothing can happen to me and suddenly I knew that I wasn't mad at him anymore.

Later we cooked together, our father cooked with the three of us and we made spaghetti, our usual, but now and then I leaned into him and he would give me a quick hug, but I felt that he was there if I needed him. If I fell, he would be there.

∽

Mum had put a letter in my room. It was a card with a picture of the sea on it, blue as anything.

"I love you!" was written on it. "I love you to death!" but in Italian. *"Ti amo da morire!"* So corny, but so true. And then *"Ardo d'amore per te!!"* That he was burning up with love. For me.

That's when I had to cry. Just a flash fire, I thought, and had to look it up on the internet to see what that was in Italian. *Un fuoco di paglia.*

Love is *un fuoco di paglia*, I thought, that burns so hot it consumes everything around it, until nothing is left except ashes, and even just a few of those.

∽

We phoned each other again.

He talked about the sea again and that I had to come. That it was so incredible, so truly incredible, so soft, so smooth, like a velvet blanket, a blue velvet blanket.

Eventually, he wanted to go back forever, to this sea, to the Mezzogiorno. That's where he belonged, that's where he had to be, that's where he wanted to build bridges and houses like his father. His grandparents were already old, already a bit helpless, and they smelled like vanilla and grapes.

His voice came out kind of rough and breathless, and I felt close to him.

I knew, I don't know why but I knew that now I wanted to, when I saw him. I wanted it soon, to breathe in his sea air, his hair, his skin. It would be tanned from the sun, dark like his eyes, and soft.

I knew we would do it, not because everyone else did, not because that's just what you did, but because I wanted to, because I wanted it with him, in some hidden corner by the sea that he would have found, because it was beautiful and the right place.

He asked if I would come, whether that was possible, and I said, "Yes."

Yes, that it was possible.

That I would make it possible. To come. To him. That I would do it. Now.

I had to push down the tingling in my stomach, my toes, my voice, everywhere.

"Yes, I'm coming!" I wanted to shout with that tingly voice, those tingly vocal chords, but I couldn't, because everything dissolved, my vocal chords, my voice, me.

And then we were quiet.

Is this love, I asked myself, my love, the first one that I will never forget in my whole life, that will come true or not, that will last or not?

Doesn't matter, I thought. It is love. Whatever it becomes. This is it.

Suddenly I understood my parents and that they felt this same longing, and I asked myself whether he was like this with Babsi and whether she would probably go back to Rudi and I knew she should but that it wasn't my business anymore.

"Are you there?" asked Carlo through the telephone.

"Are you?"

"Yes."

"Me, too."

And then to breathe out and whisper again. "Are you still there?"

"Are you?"

"Yes."

"Me, too."

I clicked on the internet to see when the trains left for Italy.

"I'll come and meet you," Carlo said. "I'll pick you up in Venice."

"Yes!" I said. "Venice. Wait for me there and then we'll go together to your Mezzogiorno and to your sea."

"Do you feel it?" he asked. "The longing?"

"Yes. The longing."

"For what?"

"I don't know."

"For me?"

"I don't know."

"Come!" he said. "Will you come?"

∾

And then I set off. My mind empty and my mouth dry. I can't say that I wasn't scared. I was. I still am, but it's okay.

I threw a few things in my backpack, got my passport, gathered up my money, grateful at how much my parents' guilty conscience had improved my finances.

Mum was at work, my brothers at Grandma's. I left a note.

Going to Carlo. See you soon.

Then I took the streetcar across town to the train station. I bought a ticket at the counter and walked to the platform. The train came and I got on.

It was simple. Like something I did every day.

When the train left, I stood at the window and basked in the sun. Toward evening the mountains appeared through the gray. There was snow on their peaks. We hurtled straight for them, like there was no stopping.

At some point my phone rang. Mum.

For a moment I felt like I was going to fall apart, I was shaking. But when I heard her voice, I was strangely calm.

"Mum!" I said. "Hi. Don't worry. I'm going to see Carlo. I'm going to stay there until school starts. Which is pretty soon. I have everything under control. So don't worry. Say hello to everyone. I love you. You know that, right? Mum? Are you there?"

"Charlotte," she said. "What is the meaning of this? What's all this nonsense? Where on earth are you?"

"On the train!" I said, and I held my breath. "I'm on the train." I could picture her sitting in the kitchen, nibbling on a cookie or a carrot, not having a clue.

Her voice exploded like a grenade. "What?? What is that supposed to mean? You're on the train? What train? Are you kidding? You come home right this minute."

I swallowed. "That won't work. We're almost in Venice."

"What!!?"

"Almost in Venice," I repeated.

Then she hung up.

Three minutes later my phone rang again.

"What are you saying? What do you mean? Are you pulling my leg?"

"No. Really. I'm not."

The phone was silent. I held my breath.

Her voice changed. "What do you mean? What is that supposed to mean? You get on a train to Italy and you don't tell me? You just take off like that?"

"It's all okay, Mum!" I said, and for a moment I wished I was back at home, surrounded by her arms, in her smell.

"I'm doing well. I'm almost in Venice. Carlo is going to pick me up. You know him. Then we're going to drive down to the Mezzogiorno. To his grandparents' place on the Ionian Sea."

"What!?" she asked again, completely hysterical. "What? Where are you going?"

"To the Mezzogiorno. The Ionian Sea." It sounded so lovely.

She began to cry, sniffling into the phone.

"Okay," she said, and I figured she was struggling to stay calm. "Okay, good. Let's talk. Are you trying to punish us? Is that what this is about? For this past year, for the separation, for all this moving around that we've been doing? I know it hasn't been easy, not for you or the boys. But it hasn't been easy for me, either. For anyone. Are you trying to punish us for all that? And what happens now? What do you have in mind next?"

I had to smile a bit. "Oh, Mum, don't be silly. I don't have anything in mind. I just want to make out with my boyfriend. You of all people can understand that."

I knew that she would have smacked me right through the telephone if she could have. I could feel her taking a deep breath.

"Sorry, Mum, really. I'm just going to see Carlo. I'm almost sixteen, you know."

You always want to be where you aren't, and right now I wanted her to brush the hair out of my face and smooth out the frown lines above my nose, and I said she should say hi to my brothers and Dad and Grandma, all of them.

"The train's just getting in," I said. "Into Venice. Carlo is going to be there. So you shouldn't worry. He knows his way around here. He knows his way around here just like at home." I paused briefly. "We have to hang up, Mum. It will take a few hours to drive down to the Mezzogiorno. Then you can talk to Carlo's mother.

When we get there. I'll call you. I'll say hi to Carlo for you. Is that okay with you? Klara, too."

I had a feeling that she was nodding. Of course I couldn't see it for myself, but I could feel it through the phone.

"Do you have money?" she asked. "How did you pay for the train —"

It was already getting late. "I have enough money. You always gave us something."

She sighed. "I'm so sorry."

"Don't be," I said. "Everything's okay. I'm good."

"Look after yourself," she whispered. "Take care. I love you, my Charlotte Ringlotte."

"Yes. Yes, I know. I know that. Me, too."

And that was it.

∽

He was standing on the platform and looking in the wrong direction. I walked slowly toward him, my step light.

Thanks to …

… the "Schreibzeit Wien" team, especially Karin, who taught me to always take a few steps back and see things fresh.

… Paulus, who brought calm and professional clarity and assurance to me and to my text.

… Irmgard, who after many years of writer's block brought me gently back on course and stoked the fire with astute thoughtfulness.